IZZY HARVEY:

Rise of the Falcons

~

JAMES HEWLETT

Cover design by Martelia Design. Logo, Icons, appendices and visuals/imagery by Anthony Barbapiccola.

First published by Burton Mayers Books 2025

ISBN- **9781917224147**
Typeset in Garamond

www.BurtonMayersBooks.com

For Robyn

The girl who lights up every heart, brings a smile to every face and leaves an imprint on every soul she meets.

ACKNOWLEDGMENTS

Reading isn't important because it helps you to get a job. It's important because it gives you the room to exist beyond the reality you are given. It is how humans merge. It is how minds connect. Dreams, empathy, understanding and escapism. Reading is love in action. Reading is taking the chance to create some peace in a world of noise, stillness in the chaos of hectic.

When I first started writing 'Jack Harvey – Breakthrough,' my dream was to write a book that my children could relate to. For them to believe in and to be inspired by. Be inspired by both the characters in the book and the fact that their dad could turn his dream into something tangible. I never in my wildest imaginations thought that my journey would see a second, let alone my third book published. I have met some incredible people who have guided and inspired my journey in the literary world and continue to encourage me to put words on a page.

Where do I start with the thank-you's? As a male and someone who played football extensively, the thought of fighting football prejudice never really entered my head. My older brother played. My mates all played club and school. It was expected of us. Not once was I called vicious evil names for playing a sport, a game. But after speaking to sportswomen for a bit of research, I was shocked that this kind of behaviour was going on. And despite the rise in the Women's Premier League and the success of England's Lionesses, in some areas it still is. We still have a long way to go.

Away from the football environment, former England netball captain Pamela Cookey gave up her valuable time while on a visit to the Island. Fresh off the plane and on a Friday night, it would have been easy to have said 'no thanks' and had an early night, but she too realises that kids need inspirational characters. Whether they are ripping up the netball court for England or creating visions of new superstars as the words jump off a page into a person's mind. These people and characters all have a part to play in physical and mental health of the next generation.

I had a wonderful chat with my children's secondary school PE teacher and a former footballer whose stories fascinated me and made me sad to think that girls had such a fight simply to play the game I took for granted as a young boy. Thank you, Kat, and Hannah, you should be proud of what you achieved.

My early proof-readers, Rob, thank you for your time, encouragement and faith in the process. My family, Mum, Andrew, Ruth and Peter. Unwavering support as always. Elizabeth, who has taken on the PA side of Jack Harvey (the bit I dislike!) I couldn't do it without you. Anthony, a graphic design genius, I've never had to ask more than once, and nothing is too much trouble, thank you. There are many more cogs to the JH machine of course. My friends and Jack Harvey champions out there are too numerous to mention, but you know who you are. You have my gratitude!

One of my main drives for writing the Jack Harvey stories is to encourage literacy in kids through reading. Working with the amazing Sally Gallichan and her charity in Jersey, 'Words and Numbers Matter', showed me that the rise in the use of screens and tablets is taking that ability to read, write and construct basic sentences away from everyday use, and making it harder for kids to connect with a book. We all have a part to play to use modern tech sensibly and to keep the physical book in our lives.

I am lucky to have a supportive and enthusiastic football fan as my publisher. It was Richard of Burton Mayers Publishers who suggested I move up my time scale and bring Izzy to the forefront of the Jack Harvey series with her own story. Once again, the support I have brings my characters and my vision to the page and into your homes.

Robyn and Harvey, as always, these books are for you. I hope you have as much fun and enjoyment reading 'Rise' as I have writing it.

James Hewlett

<u>A snippet of reader testimonials for Jack Harvey.</u>

James Hewlett's second book once again ignites meaningful discussions about character development, life's highs and lows, and – and what I appreciated most - the valuable lessons sport teaches, like winning and losing with humility. It's a captivating read, and my schoolkids are now eager to dive into the next instalment.

– Welcome Bay Primary School.

I love the character traits which I can use to teach my children about themselves. Resilience, determination and perseverance, which are fundamental in life.

Exciting, fast paced and well written with the younger reader in mind. It inspires and keeps them gripped until the very end.

Fast-paced, action-packed – what more could you ask for?

I literally couldn't put it down, brilliant.

1

*Every legend begins with a dream, every victory with a
challenge. The sky belongs to those who dare to soar.
Play with passion, fight with your heart and
Rise like the falcon.*

The crowd roared again, 'Harvey, Harvey, Harvey' they chanted. The yellow and blue of the mighty Accies Ladies Football Club swarmed across the pitch, pushing forward once again. Isabelle (Izzy) Harvey, their brilliant captain leading from the front. Superstar midfielder, goal scorer, England International. Hero to millions of girls and boys all over the country, idolised across the world. The scarves, flags and banners flew all around the giant stadium. 65,000 people all singing as one ...

'Izzy?'

The tackle was won in midfield, Isabelle Harvey with an inch-perfect sliding tackle. One of the best female players on the planet, she was up and motoring away towards the goal, her hair flowing behind her like an Amazonian warrior princess. Opposition players fell off her as they desperately tried to stop her, to slow her down, in any way that they could…

'Isabelle?'

She beat one player with a drop of the shoulder, then another by pushing the ball through a defender's legs before spinning and twisting with the ball seemingly glued to her foot. She powered her way into the penalty area, just the keeper to beat; score the goal and the European Champions League was hers. She drew her famous right foot back to shoot, the same lethal right boot that had already won her the World Player of the Year for an incredible eighth time…

'ISABELLE HARVEY!'

I jumped out of my skin. Suddenly I was transported away from the game, whisked from my imagination and sat back in my seat at school - maths with Mr Fancourt, learning multiples and fractions.

'Isabelle Harvey', the teacher announced once again, a little quieter now that he had my attention. 'I would appreciate it if you paid a little more devotion to the lesson and a little less attention to the football field!' Mr Fancourt was a great teacher, but Maths just wasn't my thing. I realised I'd been staring out the window, lost in another world. My dream of becoming the best female player on the planet would have to wait. In truth, I wanted to be the best footballer there ever was. Starring for my hometown club – The Accies - and becoming the captain of the England team - my national side - was a long way away. I wasn't even playing for my school team. We didn't even have a school football team, at least the girls didn't. It wasn't for lack of trying though.

Our PE teacher and the football coach was a man called Mr Roger Smith. A man who took pride in telling us all he had been a teacher for 40 years. We didn't believe him. We were convinced he had been a teacher for at least 140 years. Yes, he was old, but his views on football were so out of touch. At least I thought so. He refused to pick anyone for the school team unless they were boys. I knew I was better than some, if not all of the boys currently turning out for the Falcon Hill School. But I was still forced to sit and watch as they went through training with Smith and played their games at the weekend. We were encouraged to attend, to show school spirit and support our class-mates.

I wanted to play. It was so unfair.

I would go home and look at my big brother Jack. Jack had been signed as an academy player by the Accies Football Club. Once one of the greatest clubs in England and one of the best in Europe until a few years ago when they fell on some hard times. Jack was already getting paid to play for the junior sides! Well, an allowance at least. At 16 he had all his kit paid for, including the latest pair of brightly coloured boots that were all the rage in the Premier League. He had free tracksuits, training kits, tee shirts, shorts; anything he wanted he just had to ask the kitman for it and he'd get it.

'Dad,' I cried out, 'it's so unfair. I work just as hard as Jack, and he gets all that stuff for free! I don't get anything.'

'I know, Iz,' he replied. 'I know it's tough for you. One day you will get your rewards, you have to keep working hard, keep practicing.'

Dad had already written to Mr Smith, and to the headteacher, Mr Thomas Blackthorpe, about the lack of a girls' team. Blackthorpe loved his sport but seemed more interested in rugby than football which meant that they got all the good kit, whilst the football team made do with a few cones and some bibs.

The girls' sports teams got even less. This made me cross.

'We work just as hard as the boys, harder in fact,' I argued with Mr Smith. 'Why do they get all the good stuff, and we get nothing?'

'Miss Harvey,' replied an aloof Mr Smith, 'that's just the way it is. Get used to it.'

No, Sir!' I replied abruptly, 'I will not get used to it. It's not right,' I exclaimed as I stomped off, Smith desperately trying to catch me to give me a telling off. He wouldn't catch me and would probably have forgotten by dinner time anyway. I was a girl and in his world, we didn't matter. At least, that's how we all felt.

My brother Jack was once the sporting superstar of the school. Football, athletics, swimming, he was incredible at all of it. He did play a bit of rugby, out on the wing where he could use his incredible speed, but like me, football was his love and once he had signed a schoolboy contract with the mighty Accies he was not allowed to play rugby again, in case he got injured. It didn't stop him from winning all the sprinting championships though. Like me, he had been blessed with our mum's electric speed. She was a Great British sprinter when she was younger, making the Olympic team as a junior. She was super-fast and destined for the very top before she had a really bad knee injury and never regained her top speed again.

The school term and indeed the year was fast coming to a close. The summer holidays weren't far away now which was great, but it meant that we would have to sit and watch Blackthorpe and Smith ruin another season of football by not picking me and my friends, just because we were girls.

It was so frustrating. I walked out of the big double doors at the front of the school to meet up with my best mate Tayla. Tayla also loved playing football, and like me was incredibly frustrated that we weren't allowed to play a competitive match. We had grown up on the same street, our parents were friends so hung out from an early age. We got on famously and would watch every football match we could, either live or on the TV, dissecting every goal.

We sat on the big grass bank that sloped from the front of the old Victorian building that doubled up as both a sports hall and canteen, down to the lush green sports pitch. It was used mostly for rugby matches, so the grass was long, too long for football. It did not allow for much passing football, so the games were not great to watch.

The boys' football team had surprised most people by reaching the next round of the regional championship but were now 0-6 down at half-time. The team had some good individual players, but they weren't a good team. They didn't pass the ball well to each other, and no one took the leadership role which was vital in all successful sports teams. Despite nearly the whole school turning out on a lovely sunny afternoon, we lost. Badly. It looked like it would continue to be another whole season of us sitting on that grass bank watching the boys lose, instead of playing.

Falcon Hill was not a private school, but despite the lack of funding it still looked like an amazing school, on the outside at least. And the sports facilities were ok too. But inside the school was old and tired. All the local investment seemed to go to the big private school on the hill. Millbrook House School and its associated sports section, Millbrook House Sports Academy, took all the best sporting girls in the area. They came from all over the country to study at, and to represent the school. It was without a doubt one of the best schools in the country. It was a huge building set in the grounds of an old historic castle making it look even more impressive. Only the giant structure of the Accies football stadium a few miles away broke the gaze. Your eyes were drawn into the school with its huge twin towers at the front gates and the oversized purple and gold flags flying high and proud from the old ramparts. The initials MBH, written in gold, could be seen for miles around. I could only dream of going to that school. Wearing the purple uniform with its expensive golden trim, the MBH badge proudly worn on my chest as I was running out on one of the many full-sized sports pitches that had a dedicated groundsman for each one. Rugby, hockey, basketball and netball courts next to an all-weather surface. The Olympic-sized swimming pool was next to a building where there was another indoor pool with high diving facilities, often used by current and future Olympians. The main football pitch with its lush green grass inside a large, seated area was surrounded by super bright floodlights that made you feel like it was a summer's day, even when the sky was inky black.

There were even horse stables and an arena for show-jumping attached to the academy for those girls who were good at equestrian events. All this, even before you saw the vast Victorian-styled gardens - which were immaculate - even with deer and other woodland wildlife regularly making appearances. I once had the privilege of a guided tour. Dad had managed to sneak an invite to their open day, even though I knew we could never afford such gigantic school fees. It was a stunning building; the original features of the great castle were everywhere. The students ate in what was the magnificent banquet hall, under great wooden beams which held up a ceiling covered in pictures of mythical beasts and great warriors of a forgotten time. We were surrounded by historic paintings, carved figureheads and shields. Stained-glass windows cast multi-coloured patterns during the day and shone brightly at night. It was an extraordinary set-up and one I dreamed of being involved in night after night.

The running and athletics track was occasionally used for Great Britain team training before big events. I had managed to get into one of the sprinting championships on that track, where I was narrowly beaten by a much older girl from Millbrook House, but not by much. It was somewhere I could very much imagine myself being able to go to, but only in my dreams; only a very select few girls were lucky enough to receive sporting scholarships.

I didn't enjoy school. I found some lessons a bit boring. I just wanted to be outside kicking a football, playing sports, running, climbing and jumping. I guess I just wasn't inspired enough. But my outlet was sport, even with a rubbish sports teacher who seemed to ignore the girls and our achievements. It was not something I saw changing anytime soon.

It was only during the last school assembly of the year that my attention finally peaked.

Blackthorpe had waffled on about something boring for at least half an hour. Most of us had switched off and my gaze had once again been drawn to the window, as I went back to my daydreams of becoming a professional footballer. My attention wavered from playing for England in the World Cup Final for a moment and I drifted back into the room, catching the end of a sentence that made my heart skip a beat.

'And so, after a career of 41 years as a teacher, Mr Smith will be retiring as your sports teacher,' announced Blackthorpe.

My jaw hit the floor.

'Finally!' I cried out loud and then instantly shrunk into myself as everyone including an angry Smith turned to look in my direction. My friends giggled all around me.

'As I was saying,' continued Blackthorpe, 'Mr Smith will be very much missed. We will announce his replacement over the summer holidays. But let's give Mr Smith one last Falcon Hill School round of applause for all his hard work, and the rest of us we will see you all for the new school year in September.'

I clapped hard, not because I liked Smith, but because I was excited that perhaps I might get a chance in the school team if we got a new sports teacher who understood the game. I grabbed my best friend Tayla as soon as we were dismissed.

'This could be our chance,' I said excitedly. 'We need a teacher who isn't afraid to pick girls in the school team.'

'We need a teacher who will put together a football team for the girls, but who would do that?' Tayla asked. 'What football coach would want to come here? Blackthorpe won't get a female teacher, will he? He will bring in another useless coach who won't care about us.'

'Have faith, Tayla,' I replied as the bell for

our next lesson sounded. 'I've got a really good feeling about this. This could be the start of something big for us.'

I was back into my daydreams almost as soon as our history teacher began to explain something about Vikings. I actually enjoyed history, but not today. Today I was Isabelle Harvey. School captain. Charging through the midfield to score the winning goal in the cup final.

Success isn't just winning - it's about growing. Give your best. That's the real victory.

The summer break flew past far too quickly, as the holidays always seemed to do. No matter how long we were off school, it never quite seemed enough. Both mum and dad had to work for a lot of the time we were off school, so Jack and I were left on our own, although we didn't mind.

Everyone knew where to find the two of us, down the park kicking a football around. As Jack was the older of the two of us, I was always desperately playing catch up. He was bigger, faster and stronger than me, but he never beat me easily. I made sure of that. Day after day he would celebrate winning the small-sided matches we played in. It didn't help that he always had his mate Lucas in goal. Lucas was also on the Accies books as an academy player, so even if I beat Jack, beating Lucas was another hurdle altogether. I had Tayla, and any other random wanderer who appeared at the park, whether they wanted to play or not. I was good at convincing people to join in.

We did have a two-week break together. My dad loved beach holidays and was always desperate to get away from his job. We usually ended up on a sunny island in the Mediterranean somewhere. We ate loads, too much probably. But it always ended with us having fun by the hotel pool or on the beach. Jack was seen by one of the hotel reps having a kick about by himself and managed to get roped into a 5-a-side tournament. Clearly, I wasn't going to let him have all the fun, and despite the protests that I was 'just a little girl,' and 'not strong enough to play with the boys,' Jack insisted that I join his team, of course, much to the disgust of the three others who he had been put with. There was no way I was going to put up with that attitude and told them that if they didn't like it, they could go back to the pool. You should've seen the look on their faces as they were put in their place by 'the little English girl'. I thought it was hilarious. Jack was giggling behind them, and it was hard not to laugh as they shuffled off to start the match muttering something in Spanish.

After one game they had all changed their opinion as Jack and I ran the show. We both scored bucket-loads of goals and conceded none. We won every game we played. We beat a bunch of local boys easily in the final and at the end of it, everyone wanted to come and talk to us about football. No one minded that I was a 'little English girl' now. They wanted to know all about where we came from and who we played for. We were certainly the talk of the hotel for the rest of our holiday.

We had not long been back home, in fact Jack's suitcase was still untouched - no surprise there - when an email from the school pinged into my Mum's inbox entitled; 'New Sports Teacher.'

Mum read it out breathlessly and excitedly – 'After a long search, Falcon Hill School is delighted to announce that the replacement sports teacher for the departing Mr Smith will be Miss Rachel Hunter. Miss Hunter is a brand-new teacher coming from a successful sports background, and we hope her enthusiasm will rub off on our students.'

'Hunter, mum?' I interrupted. 'Rachel Hunter the footballer?'

'It can't be,' Mum replied. 'Last I heard she had retired from football because of an injury... Izzy?' she called. I was already up in my room and onto the internet searching for 'Rachel Hunter'.

Rachel was a former England international, a midfield superstar who had played for the very best teams across Europe. She had a wand of a right foot, seemingly able to pass the ball to wherever she wanted with ease. She was so graceful and elegant. A regular in the England national side, captaining her country on occasions, playing and winning championships for the top sides in Spain, Italy and England before a horrendous tackle broke her ankle in multiple places. She nearly lost her foot, before emergency surgery had saved her. She made attempts at a comeback, but she was not the same player, and it had ended her professional playing career. She tried her hand at a bit of coaching, but there was no mention of her becoming a teacher. I was off, out the door, running down the road to see my best mate, Tayla.

I was through the front door shouting, 'Hi' to her parents, as I zoomed up the stairs and into Tayla's bedroom. She too was on the internet and a picture of Rachel Hunter scoring an overhead kick in a cup final was on her screen as I barged in.

'You've heard!' I cried.

Tayla was glued to the screen and didn't even need to look up to know I was there. Our bond was instinctive. We had followed the same routine for as long as we could both remember, ever since we were paired up for a three-legged race at pre-school. She was the only one who could keep pace with me as we won by a mile. We had been firm friends ever since.

'Yes, I didn't believe it,' Tayla replied. 'My mum said it's her. She needed to take a job as a teacher and no other local school would take her without any experience. Blackthorpe's wife is a massive fan and told him to hire her as a sports teacher immediately,' she laughed. We both did. It was a funny image. Big, scary, grizzled headteacher Mr Blackthorpe, doing exactly what his wife told him! We sat and discussed the career of Rachel Hunter and what she might bring to Falcon High School. With her background, surely, she would want to have a girl's football team.

For the first time ever, I longed for the summer holidays to end and get back to school – to play football.

*Skill has never been just the product of coaching —
It's born from a deep, unbreakable bond between a
child and a ball, a love affair that turns practice into
passion and dreams into reality.*

For the first time ever, I was excited to go back to school after the long summer holiday. I sidestepped the entrance to my form room and went straight to the PE department. A big sign was placed on the sports noticeboard. Miss Hunter had stuck the A4 notice bang in the middle, so it was impossible to miss.

'Girls football try-outs tonight. All years welcome'

It was music to my ears. ALL YEARS WELCOME.

'At last,' Tayla said. 'We will get a chance to show what we can do.' I raced home after a whirlwind first day at school to grab my boots, sending my dad spinning as I darted up the stairs to Jack's room.

'Hey Iz', he said. 'Dad told me your news, that's awesome. Go and smash it,' he smiled.

I jogged back the short distance to the school gates and found Tayla who was already waiting for me. Like me, she loved the game, was super-fast and very clever. She was what I described as book-smart. She read something and just understood it; sometimes, if I read something, it may as well have been written in a foreign language. I'd have to re-read and break it all down. Tayla just got it. But she was my best mate and we both loved training and hanging out together.

We got ourselves changed and headed out onto the pitch. Stood directly in front of us were two girls, Sophie Thompson and Leila Dos Santos. I'd seen Sophia play before. She always looked tired for some reason, but she was a great player. She had a nice energy about her and was always talking on the pitch, where to go, who to mark and when to pass. She was what Rachel Hunter would later describe to us as a 'natural leader'. The other girl, Leila, was a tough-looking Brazilian girl. She spoke broken English with a heavy Latin accent. She didn't even acknowledge Tayla or me as we walked past, she was content with doing keepy-ups and flicks with a plastic bottle top! She clearly could play!

Leila had been obsessed with football since she could walk. Growing up in a football-mad family in the bustling city of Rio de Janeiro, her father coached the local boys' team. Football in South America is a religion, and her family lived for the game. She was always on the sidelines, absorbing everything. At the age of 7, she was already competing in boys' leagues in Brazil, because there were no girls' teams in her neighbourhood. At 10 years old her dad moved the family to the UK, and she found herself unable to find a team in the area as the boys' teams didn't allow girls to join them, and when she did manage to sneak on having cut her hair short to pretend she was a boy, she was quickly found out and sent off. She now saw Rachel's appointment as the sports coach as her chance to shine.

Shine she certainly did. Everyone tried hard, as we all wanted to impress the new coach. She ghosted past countless other girls who seemed unable to get the ball off her. I was lucky that she was on my team, so I didn't have to try and tackle her. I was marking Sophia though, who was running the game for the other side. I was desperate to influence the game but try as I might, it just didn't click. My passing was off, nothing fell right for me. I ran hard but got nowhere. Leila didn't pass the ball to me, (or anyone else either) even when I was in good positions. But my first touch wasn't clean. I just couldn't control the ball like I was used to. I caught Tayla's eye towards the end of the first half. Tayla was on the other side and was having a decent game.

'Relax, Izzy,' she said.' You're trying too hard.'

'Nothing is going right' I said, my eyes welling up.

'Iz, you've put so much pressure on yourself to do well. Just let the ball do the work. Don't force it. Use your speed, you know you can do this.'

Moments later, the ball came over and just as I was about to bring it under control, Tayla whipped it off my toe and was away. 'Sorry,' she cried out as she flew past.

'Great, Tayla,' cried Rachel. 'Really great.' Even my best friend was making me look silly now. I know she didn't mean to. I just needed something to go my way. I ran hard into the second half, telling myself that something had to go right soon, and then, just as I was beginning to lose hope, a run and shot by Leila was blocked and the ball ran to me; I was running at full speed and about to unleash my best shot, but as I was about to strike the ball it hit a tiny bobble. It wasn't much but just enough to move the connection point and as I was going so fast, I was unable to react and could only watch the ball, as my shot sailed miles over the bar. I'd blown it.

The game was over a few minutes later. I ran off the pitch, grabbed my clothes and was out the door before anyone else came in. Tears streamed down my face as I ran down the road, still in my boots, into the house, into my room and then I dived under the covers just in time for the flood of tears to arrive.

I lay there alone for ages and quietly cried until I fell asleep.

The next thing I knew I was getting a prod. 'Izzy, Izzy, get up, what ARE you doing?' Jack was there looking surprised that I was still in my grubby football kit – boots and all.

'Jack, I had a stinker. I was rubbish. Nothing went right. I'll never make the team now,' I cried again. The tears coming thick and fast again.

'Iz, you wanted it so badly. You put yourself

under too much pressure. Come on,' he said. 'We're going out.'

'Where? 'I asked.

'The park,' he replied. 'I'm meeting Lucas. You're coming too.'

Reluctantly, I dragged myself down to the park and began half-heartedly kicking the ball with Jack. I began to relax as I listened to the terrible jokes and utter boy nonsense Jack and Lucas were telling each other. Before I knew it, I'd forgotten about the trial match, and as a pass from Jack sat up nicely in front of me, I struck it hard towards the goal. It fizzed along the ground and past Lucas before he could react. A big smile came over my face.

'That's better little Sis,' Jack said. As a more than annoyed Lucas picked the ball out of the back of the net. He shot me a determined look as he set himself for the next shot, which he saved, just. But I was feeling so much better and joined in the laughing and joking until it was dark, and we trudged home for dinner.

Tomorrow, I would go again. I'd show Rachel Hunter I was a good player and that I deserved to be on the team.

In sport, there is no true failure - only lessons. Some days you win, some days you don't.

As I predicted, I didn't make Rachel's first team, which didn't surprise me. What was more upsetting was that I wasn't even a sub. What chance did I have of impressing her if I couldn't even get on the pitch.

I went along to watch anyway. If I couldn't change anything on the pitch, I was determined that I wouldn't be left out altogether. Rachel saw me and smiled.

'Nice to see you here to support Isabelle,' she said. I smiled back, even though I was frustrated. I was still in awe of Miss Hunter. She had represented her country after all. Even in the warm-up, you could see she had an incredible first touch and she was so fast to move the ball it seemed to be a blur. It was the first time I had been that close to someone so good. I couldn't help but wonder if she still could play, even after that injury.

The match itself was over almost before it had started. Having one or two great players was good, but if the rest of the team didn't know what to do, what hope did we have? We were one down only a few seconds into the match. Their first shot went in after a mistake from our keeper. As did their second and third. We quickly realised we needed someone who wasn't afraid to play in goal.

The goals kept coming, and even the best efforts of Tayla, Sophia and Leila couldn't stem the tide. I had lost count of the goals before half-time; it was painful to watch and the girls coming off looked upset. I went over to console a few of them after the game. Tayla especially, who had defended well but was left on her own for a lot of the game.

'We need you Izzy,' she said. 'I'm going to tell Miss Hunter she was wrong, and we need you in the team.

'Thanks mate,' I said. I'm going to show her I deserve a place in this team.

The next day at training I arrived early and

was last to leave. I took my ball so I could carry on after all the kit had been cleared away. I saw Rachel sitting in her car watching me for a few minutes before she drove home. I did the same in the next session and the next. First to arrive, last to leave. Running harder, listening to everything Rachel was saying, absorbing every last drop of her information. I began to cycle to the pitch, so I could go for a quick ride afterwards. Dad warned me not to do too much, not to overdo it, but I was focused. 'I'm getting into the team Dad,' I said.

'Rachel can't keep me out forever'.

'I know,' Dad said. 'I know, she won't. Not if you keep working as hard as you do.'

Friday morning arrived. Rachel put the team sheet up first thing on a Friday so we would see the team as soon as we arrived at school. The boys' team was there also, but for once I paid no attention to it, I was focused on the girl's number 8 – Isabelle Harvey. I was the only one there since I had arrived 30 minutes early for lessons. I couldn't wait to see the team sheet.

'Yes!' I cried out, spinning around and bumping into the figure standing behind me.

'Well done, Isabelle.' It was Rachel. 'Your hard work didn't go unnoticed; you deserve your chance. Just relax and don't try too hard to force things. You are a natural footballer. I'll see you tomorrow morning, bright and early I'm sure,' she said with a smile.

The game, my first for the school, was not how I dreamt it. I ran and ran. I tackled hard. But like the game before, we were just outgunned. They had players who could play in every position.

We had changed our goalkeeper, but our fortunes were the same. We were down and out before the first half had ended. At least in the second half, we stemmed the tide. We even scored a goal. Tayla put in a great tackle and my hurried clearance fell nicely for Leila, who raced away past some half-hearted defending and scored a consolation goal.

We were all aware we had players missing in some key areas. Without new recruits we stood no chance. Even with Rachel's enthusiasm on the training pitch, we knew we needed to go and find players for her and get them to the training sessions.

Rachel and I had a long chat after our next training session. We both identified that we needed to find a goalkeeper as a priority, as well as another three or four girls who could play.

'I'll find someone,' I told her. 'I'm sure we can get a decent team together.'

'I believe you, Izzy,' she replied. 'If anyone has the determination to do it, clearly it's you!'

I knew there was no way we could enter the national schools' cup if we were missing players in those key areas. We needed reinforcements. I set about making up posters for the team, something Leila just laughed at.

'Who do you think is going to read that?' she said. I ignored her. I was on a mission.

It was after our next Saturday morning match that I spotted Charley. Charlotte Caldwell was a tough-looking kid. Both her older brothers played rugby for the school. Her dad had even had professional trials when he was younger, so rugby was in the family blood. When her brothers needed to practice, they got Charley to join in. She toughened up quickly and became a half-decent rugby player herself, but she preferred football. Her tough tackling sent many of the boys scuttling off in a different direction when we crashed one of their playground games.

'Charley', I said to her during our art lesson. 'Do you fancy playing for the school football team? I think you'd be a brilliant defender.'

She was painting a seashore scene, with

dramatic crashing waves, spray firing up high in the air. Like me, she was a creative personality, in complete contrast to the image she gave out on the sports field. Her eyes lit up.

'You want me to come and play?' she said. 'I'd love to. I didn't think Blackthorpe allowed girls to play at school?'

'Miss Hunter has changed all that. If you are good enough, you can play.'

Sophia Thompson had joined in the conversation. She didn't like art, so she was just wandering around, pretending to look for some paint, even though she had every colour she needed.

'Come and join us,' she said, 'and bring anyone else who fancies a game too.'

'I might just know someone,' she said. 'My best mate Maya likes football too but is a bit shy.'

'Maya the gymnast?' I said. I had seen her before doing her flips and tumble turns. Everyone knew who Maya was. Walking around with her shoes on her hands and her legs high in the air, it was her party trick. But no one seemed to know her very well. She was quiet in lessons.

'Yes', Charley said. 'She used to be a

goalkeeper when we were younger, until her parents told her she had to concentrate on her gymnastics. But I know she would love to come back and play again. I'll come along to training and make sure she comes, too.' I looked at Sophia and smiled. A goalkeeper, perfect!

Word quickly got around that Sophia and I were recruiting for the school team. All of a sudden people were lining up to join. Having a former professional player as a coach had become a massive draw for those who would otherwise have gone and played different sports elsewhere.

Robyn Brooks, the niece of Accies legendary striker Dexter Brooks, joined our recruiting team. Robyn had football in her blood. Uncle Dexter (or Dex) was the Accies' all-time leading scorer and until recently had played for England. Robyn had been going to Accies games with her dad to watch Uncle Dex since she was old enough to walk. She knew everything there was to know about the Accies. If I thought Dad and Jack were Accies fanatics, they were amateurs when matched up against Robyn. She was so enthusiastic about the game it made other girls come along just to see what the fuss was all about, to have some fun of their own. I'd known Robyn since pre-school and we'd always got on well. She loved playing and dreamed like me of being a professional footballer, like her uncle.

Poppy Renner was the next on our 'hit list'. We collared her in a PE lesson. Poppy grew up in a very wealthy family where her parents expected her to pursue "respectable" hobbies like ballet or piano. Poppy had spent a couple of years at an expensive private boarding school overseas, but she hated it, so very reluctantly her parents pulled her out and enrolled her at Falcon Hill. But Poppy was always drawn to football. She admitted to us that she used to watch matches in secret and played alone in the garden when her parents were out or at work.

'My parents will disapprove of this, please don't tell them,' she said. 'They think it's not a sport for girls like me. Football is a boy's sport apparently, at least according to them.'

'Rubbish!' Rachel had overheard our conversation and had wandered over. 'Football is for everyone, Boys and girls. That's the beauty of this game. Anyone can play. They have football-tots for the tiny ones, they have walking football for the oldest ones, I've even seen a game for people who have lost a leg, and they use special crutches. It's an amazing sight. If your mum and dad have a problem with you playing football, tell them to come and speak to me.'

Tess Moreno had been listening in. Tess was an exchange student from Portugal. She was only living in England for a year and hadn't really settled. Her parents had told her to join every club she could to make some friends. She thought football would be a fun way to meet people.

'That sounds cool,' she said in a very strong Portuguese accent. 'Can I come along, too?'

'Of course,' we all replied happily.

Rachel had been busy herself and turned up to that evening's training session with a tall girl, Amara Ratcliffe. I knew Amara was an amazing long jump and high jumper.

'She could be an amazing defender,' I said to Sophia. As the team captain, Sophia was seeing how much effort I was putting into the team both on and off the pitch and we were becoming good friends.

'Yes, I think you are right, she can run, jump. She's tall and wow!' she exclaimed, as we watched Amara kick a ball from one side of the pitch into the sand pit on the far side. 'She can certainly kick a ball too!'

We had 18 girls at our next training session. Not everyone would be able to make the team, but it was double the amount from the week before and now had the makings of a good team, if we were able to play together.

We had Maya Kinsey in goal,

Charley Caldwell, Tayla Kelly, Amara Radcliffe and Ava Carrington were our defenders.

Robyn Brooks, Sophia Thompson, Tess Moreno and me in the midfield, with Leila Dos Santos and Poppy Renner as our two strikers.

We were one girl short of what I thought would be a great team. Tess was a nice girl, but football wasn't her true love. She tried hard for us, but even she said she only came to have fun with her new friends, and she never really found her groove, even though she seemed happy to be with us.

Barriers will always stand in your way until you are ready to push past them.

Training was good for the next few weeks; we played a couple of matches. One against the younger boys from our school, we lost. As hard as we tried, we just weren't very well organised. The next game was against a school from the next county. Again, we all worked hard. Rachel was trying to explain to us that we didn't always have to attack, but we all wanted to score goals and pushed forward. What it did mean though, was that there were a lot of goals in our games. Leila could shoot, there was no doubting that, and Sophia could play too. Today though, she looked tired. Some days she was great, others not so. Something wasn't quite right with her, but she was always smiling on the football pitch, so I let it go.

It ended in another defeat, the girls seemed happy though. They were all still upbeat in the changing rooms afterward. We knew these games were just a bit of fun and as we were all so new to playing proper matches, we knew we were still learning. But I didn't like losing. Never did. Whether it was a football match, at training, board games or card games, I needed to win. And in a household where we had a dad who refused to let us win, a former Olympian mother and a super competitive bigger brother it was tough. Any success I had, I knew I'd earned it.

As I was leaving training, I saw one of the new girls at school standing over by the little stand that sat in the middle of the pitch – we called it a stand, even though there were only two rows of seats. Blackthorpe had it made so he could sit and watch his boys play rugby on a Sunday morning. It was Zara Van Der Meer, watching us intently. I was sure she was smoking a cigarette, or a vape or something, she had her school tie half undone, shirt hanging out and skirt rolled up way too high. She came with a reputation of being a tough, bad girl. Her parents were well off, but never around, always at work, often out of the country. Zara was looked after by a nanny when she was at home, which she hated. She was a former student of Millbrook House, but she rebelled at every opportunity. She had been bullied about being 'the rich kid,' even at Millbrook House. Her parents were regular visitors to the school office when they were back in England. Zara was given a last warning when she came in late again with her hair dyed blue, her fingernails painted black and wearing her favourite chunky boots instead of school shoes. She had a huge argument with a teacher and had climbed out of a window whilst in another detention.

The breaking point came when she was caught smoking on school grounds with some older kids from a different school that she had let in through a fire escape. She was expelled from the school, much to the disgust of her parents who refused to fly home from their holiday in the Maldives, leaving the fallout to be dealt with by their hired help. Zara joined Falcon Hill and immediately started to cause trouble. Everyone knew who she was before she had even joined. So here she was hanging about on her own down at the pitch, perhaps about to cause more trouble. I was nervous about talking to her.

I took a big deep breath and walked over with Tayla and Robyn next to me for moral support.

'Hi,' I said. 'I'm Izzy.'

'And?' she replied.

'We, er, I don't think, we have met yet' I stuttered. 'I just wanted to come and say hello. This is my friend Tayla and...'

'Ok,' she said, cutting me off, 'see ya then,' and turned back to her vape.

I turned to leave, but something stopped me.

'You know Vaping is really bad for you, and probably illegal for someone your age,' I blurted out.

'No one cares, Izzy,' she said. 'No one gives a...'

'Hey!' came a loud cry cutting her off mid-sentence, 'Are you smoking over there?' A man in a sharp black suit was storming across the pitch.

'Oh no', Tayla cried, 'it's Blackthorpe.'

'Run', I said to Zara. 'He won't recognise you from over there, run, we will cover for you.'

Zara looked at me puzzled but then turned and ran like the wind towards the hedge, swerving round a bench before disappearing through a gap in a flash.

Wow, I thought, she could move.

Blackthorpe arrived puffing.

'Who was that?' He demanded.

'No idea sir,' I said. 'I thought it was one of the kids from Saint Vic's School who came to spy on training, and we went to tell them to leave.'

'Ah, well done girls. Good school spirit, yes, well done,' he said as he turned and headed back quickly towards his office where he would be on the phone immediately to Saint Victoria's school to complain to anyone who would listen.

Tayla and I walked back to collect our bags and go home, and as we turned, I caught sight of Zara's face. She was still hiding behind one of the huge Oak trees that flanked the playing fields.

'Thank you,' she mouthed towards me. I smiled and gave her the 'Ok' sign.

We had PE the next day, and Zara was in the class with us. Miss Hunter started with a mini-speech about sports and discipline and how sport was meant to be fun, but we still had to set standards for ourselves. Zara for once was paying attention, and soon we saw why. She was a proper baller. She could play.

She robbed the ball off the toe of Sophia and accelerated past Leila - who was no slouch - before thumping the ball past the ever-improving Maya in goal. She turned and looked at me.

'You got room in your team for one more?' she said.

'Only if you stop vaping,' I said bravely. 'It's disgusting, and it makes you smell funny!' I smiled.

Zara laughed. 'Yeah ok. Didn't like it anyway.' We became friends from that moment, even though I didn't like the way she behaved sometimes; my mum kept telling me how hard it was for her not to have her parents around. Despite having money to buy whatever she wanted, all she wanted was to have her parents around to talk to, to have dinner with and to watch her play football. I realised that I was the lucky one. Despite sometimes feeling like Jack was the footballing priority, my dad was always at my matches. He loved the game, any game. Whether it was the mighty Accies when they were at the peak of their powers, or walking our dog past a park pitch when he would stop to watch 10 minutes of 'FC Random' versus 'NoIdeaWhoYouAre United.'

Zara was a very good player, but she was right on the edge. Her first game with us against St Beders High School was spectacular. She ran the show with Sophia. Her passing was excellent. Between her and Charley the opposition was getting roughed up – but fairly. Charley was not scared of a tackle and was going in hard, but she would win the ball (mostly) and didn't give away many free kicks. Zara wasn't afraid of anyone. She scored our first goal, curling the ball neatly into the bottom corner after a period where we refused to let St Beders have a touch. She set up the second for Leila just before half-time for 2-0. The second half was just moments old when she picked up a yellow card for a wild challenge on a girl who previously said something mean to her.

Rachel had no choice but to substitute her off not long after that, when she had lost control of her emotions and was in danger of being sent off. She was upset, shouting after the other girl.

After she went off, we lost a bit of control and they pulled a goal back, but late on, as they pressed for an equaliser, I managed to win a tackle and my long clearance turned into a great pass for the flying Ava, who rolled the ball across the box for Poppy to smash home!

Our first win! We were all delighted. Rachel had the biggest smile on her face. 'Well done girls. I am so happy for you. We deserved that; you've all worked so hard. Now off you go and enjoy the rest of your weekend.'

The strongest people find the courage and caring to help others, even if they are going through their own storm.

The weekend flew past in a heartbeat and before I knew it, I was sat in class listening to Miss Braithwaite talking about rocks in our geography lesson. There was an empty chair though. No Zara. She wasn't in our next lesson either, or the one after. I sent her a message at the end of the day to see if she was ok.

The reply shocked me:

'Hey Iz, I got suspended again. That annoying girl from St Beders saw me after the game and called me a spoilt little rich girl. So, I punched her. Her parents told Blackthorpe and now I'm not allowed to play for the school anymore...'

'Oh no Za, why did you hit her?' I replied

'I don't know. I hate being called names like that. I'm so cross with myself though, and now I can't play for the team.'

First thing next morning I was knocking on the door of Miss Hunters' office.

'Hi Izzy,' she said. 'I know why you are here. It's about Zara, isn't it?'

'Yes,' I said, 'it's so unfair, that girl was being mean to her all game. It's not fair. We need Zara in the team,' I blurted it all out at 100 miles an hour.

'Whoa there Izzy, take a breath,' Rachel said. 'I don't like what the other girl did either, but you can't lose your temper and hit people. There is no option. Zara cannot play on this team whilst she shows that behaviour. We are a girls' team struggling to make an impression on a headteacher who would much rather we leave football to the boys. If we all behaved like that, he will stop us from playing any match at all. I'm sorry Izzy. Unless she shows a big improvement in behaviour I cannot pick her again.'

Zara was back at school a few days later, and whilst we were out training after lessons had finished, Blackthorpe made her sit in the hall in detention, knowing full well that she could see us and it would make her even more upset and cross with herself. It was meant to teach her a lesson, but I thought it was cruel. Zara was just really frustrated. Her parents hadn't even come back that weekend to watch her play as they decided to stay wherever they had been for work and 'have another holiday,' as Zara had sarcastically said, whilst the nanny looked after her.

I saw her speaking to Rachel a few times in the next few weeks, but she missed our next game, and the one after that too – we lost both. We tried hard but we missed her presence. Sophia too was off her game. She missed the first game, nobody seemed to know why, and she was late for the second, arriving after the game had started.

Sophia had been late for school every day in the last week, and now Blackthorpe was giving her a hard time.

'Miss Hunter was quite clear with all of you,' he said. 'To be successful in anything, you need to be disciplined. If you can't make it to school on time, then how are you going to manage in a real job when you leave school?'

He continued, 'Maybe you need to sit in the hall with Zara instead of training?' he said with a stern look.

'I'm sorry Mr Blackthorpe,' Sophia said fearfully, 'it won't happen again.'

I was confused. Sophia as the captain was supposed to set the example. On the pitch she was brilliant. So good at organising and we all looked up to her. Something was up. Tayla had noticed it too, and we watched her hurry off after the game. Usually, she stayed to chat football, but lately she had left as soon as practice was finished. We decided to follow her. She wasn't hanging around, so we had to run to catch her up. She went straight home, so we knocked on the door.

'Hey guys,' she said, 'what's up?'

'We, we just wondered if you were ok?' Tayla asked.

She invited us in and then revealed to us that her mum now worked two jobs.

'Since my dad died, we've found it quite hard,' she said. 'Mum said if I want new football boots, I'd have to buy them myself. We glanced down at the pile of old shoes and trainers and saw her football boots were awful. Split, with missing studs and frayed laces. She continued, 'Mum needed someone to look after my two younger brothers whilst she's out, so now that's my job, and she said if I cook, clean and put them to bed whilst she is working late,

I can get a new pair for my birthday.'

Tayla and I were shocked.

'But you shouldn't have to look after your brothers. No wonder you look tired and are late for school,' I said.

'Ok,' Tayla announced, 'here's the deal. You sort out dinner for the young ones and Iz and I will tidy up for you. Where's the mop?' she said smiling.

So, we mopped and wiped and hoovered the rugs. I dusted the shelves and Tayla emptied the bins. In a few hours, the house was spotless.

'No excuse now Sophia,' I said. 'See you tomorrow for the game!'

'Thanks guys,' she said, her eyes welling up with tears. 'I won't forget this.'

We walked home exhausted from our cleaning frenzy.

'How does she manage to do all that and still get to school?' Tayla asked.

'I know,' I replied. 'I'd be more than late, I'd be fast asleep every day, especially during a Blackthorpe assembly.' We both laughed.

The next day Sophia was there early for the game. Her brother and sister were both with her and sat in the stand, watching her intently.

The game was a tight one, but Sophia was

back to her best. Organising the midfield players, tackling, passing and allowing other players to express themselves. But even though we all had a good game, it wasn't quite enough. We just couldn't score a goal, and when poor Maya dropped a deep cross, one of their strikers was able to stretch out a leg to poke the ball into the back of the net. Another defeat. It was becoming a habit.

We all enjoyed playing, but I'd had enough of losing games. Zara was still not allowed to play, but at least now she was allowed to watch the game from the stand, sat with Leila's brothers.

I saw Rachel after the game,

'Miss Hunter' I called, 'Miss, we need Zara, I'm fed up with losing matches. We could be a great team with her in it.'

I didn't realise it, but Zara was right behind me.

'Miss Hunter, I am sorry for my behaviour. It will never happen again. Please let me play again,' she begged.

'Zara,' Rachel said. 'I know it won't happen again, but it's not me you have to convince.'

'Blackthorpe,' we both said at the same time.

'Afraid so,' she said. 'Mr Blackthorpe makes the rules. If you can make him change his mind, then of course I will put you straight back in the team.'

All three of us walked round to Poppy's house. She was the cleverest girl in the team. Probably the cleverest girl in our year if we were honest.

We all chipped in as Zara hand-wrote a letter. She may have been a bit of a rebel, but her handwriting was exceptionally neat. We had decided a handwritten letter was more personal and showed she cared. It took us a few hours to get it done. Poppy's mum was fully on board with our mission and kept us topped up with drinks and snacks. She even ordered us all takeaway pizza for dinner. After we had done and had finished chatting about football tactics, she drove us all home, but not before passing by the school to drop the letter off. Mr Blackthorpe would have the letter on his office desk first thing the next day.

We sat through each and every lesson, watching the door, waiting for Blackthorpe to make an appearance. Zara was desperate to see him, but he didn't show. We left our final lesson downcast and upset for Zara.

'How long is he going to punish me for?' she asked. 'It's been weeks now.'

'Have you spoken to your parents, what did

they say?' I asked her.

'They weren't bothered,' she replied. 'Mum said if I had been suspended from school then I deserved to miss playing football. She said I should concentrate on my lessons more. She told me football is a silly game and only for boys.'

'Zara, Zara, come quick.' There was a call from down the hallway. Mia and Charley were stood at the sports notice board. Miss Hunter was just walking away, she turned and smiled at us, giving a wink to Zara.

'Zara,' cried Charley, 'you're back in the team, Blackthorpe must have read the letter!

We were all delighted, hugging each other and bouncing around in a group, shouting out 'Za-ra, Za-ra.'

We were all buzzing after that news and our training that night couldn't have gone better. We passed and tackled well. Our shooting was great. Maya was on top form. Zara was charging across the pitch like she had never been outside before, laughing and smiling. We all were.

Believe in yourself - even if you don't yet. Pretend if you must, because one day, it won't be an act anymore.

The next day we had a match against Trinity College. A school from the same county. Blackthorpe had organised for us to play up at Millbrook House School as he wanted the rugby boys to play on our pitch the same day.

I had seen their school pitches many times from afar. We all had. It was hard not to see the giant castle at the top of the hill with its oversized flags flying high in the sky. But as we snaked our way down the long gravel driveway, we were all in awe as we stared out of the windows, watching a vast array of different teams playing different sports across the enormous expanse of playing fields. Dotted around were old medieval structures that were once part of the great castle's defences, now used as seated structures or storerooms for the groundskeepers. We were all in awe as we climbed out of our battered old minibus. Millbrook House had the best of everything. Once inside our eyes got wider still.

The huge wooden boards listing all the head girls since the school had opened. Expensive looking artwork hung everywhere you looked, and rich wooden floorboards ran the length of the entrance hall down to an elegant glass trophy cabinet, stuffed full of trophies of all shapes and sizes. It looked more like an exclusive country club than school changing rooms. Each girl had her own locker, with her name in golden writing on the purple door. Her awards and achievements were listed underneath in the same gold font. They had the best of everything. The best teachers across the country wanted to come and work here as they wanted for nothing. It would have been a dream to go to this school.

With everything they offered, from schooling to their famed sports programme. The Millbrook academy had a very high percentage of students go on to play professional sports or represent their country in various events. They had obvious links to two- or three-women's professional football teams, and to play for the academy meant you had a higher chance of making it as a pro. I began to daydream, gazing round at all the plaques and crests of teams that had once played on these playing fields, mounted high up on the walls. As a result, I missed most of Rachel's team talk!

We ran out onto the pitch. It was perfect. It was like a lush green carpet, and there were no bumps or divots to be found. Each blade of grass looked like it had been individually cut by a hairdresser, rather than a mower.

Millbrook House girls had a game against Trinity College too, but they played against their A-team whilst we played their B's.

We ripped into our opposition from the start. When the ball broke to me at the edge of the penalty area early in the first half, I didn't hesitate and smashed it goalwards, the keeper didn't even see it as it whizzed into the net: GOAL. I felt good, playing in this environment clearly suited me. We passed the ball so well; I don't think it would have mattered if we had played their A-team.

Millbrook House had finished their game, a resounding win long before our game was done, and most of their players and coaches came to watch the 'scruffy kids' from the school down the road.

We didn't really care what they thought of us; we just wanted to play and enjoy this opportunity. Zara was getting a few comments thrown her way, most weren't of the kind variety either, she had clearly made a few enemies during her rebellious period at Millbrook. I could see her boiling inside, but as promised, she bottled up her frustrations - mostly - a couple of over eager challenges led to a stern ticking off from the referee. It didn't slow her, or the team down though, as a lovely cross from Poppy was nodded into the net by Leila. She treated us to a bit of a Brazilian samba right in front of the Millbrook team as her celebration. They didn't appear to be very impressed. As the Millbrook House girls began to filter out, the ball was won back by a tiring Poppy. It broke to Zara who looked around for someone to pass to, but no one was free, so she pushed the ball wide and accelerated past the defender before hitting a cross shot towards the far post. The ball sped over the perfect surface and nestled into the bottom corner of the net for 3-0. A great win, and we probably deserved more.

I was over the moon. I had played well,

scored a goal. Zara was back, clearly enjoying the surface she once had graced. We had played on that incredible Millbrook House pitch and won. It was all going so well. But the post-match chat from Rachel still was a surprise.

'Girls,' she announced. 'As you know I had a long chat this week with Mr Blackthorpe, about a few things,' she smiled at Zara, 'and he has agreed to let me enter Falcon Hill into the National Cup.'

We all exploded with a million questions all at once.

'Wait, wait!' she said. 'It's a long journey and it starts with a preliminary tournament in two weeks' time. If we get through that, then we can enter the competition proper.' Now let's get home and we can begin to prepare. If we want to do well, and play on more pitches like this one, then we need to practice harder and better than before.

If you want something you have never had, you must be willing to do something you have never done.

Training, training, training. We all stayed behind after school every night that week. The girls didn't have a choice. Only Sophia was allowed to miss a couple of the sessions to take care of her siblings. I was adamant that we would be the fittest and fastest teams there.

'We won't be beaten because we are tired,' I told Rachel who laughed.

'No, I can see that,' she replied. 'I have a few ideas for you that might be helpful,' she stated and began to reel off a list of tricks and tactics that she had learned during her time at the top. I couldn't take my eyes off her and everything she said just seemed to make complete sense. It was like someone had plugged in a supercomputer to my brain and was uploading all its info, except the computer was Rachel Hunter and the information was football tactics. My mind was bursting, but I wanted to know more and to listen to more of her stories, take on all of her advice. I knew it would be priceless information.

The preliminary tournament was simple. Three teams were entered in each group. Only one team would progress through from each group to the knockout stages. It would be against local teams, and we were worried that we would be drawn against Millbrook House, but luckily we had avoided them. We felt good going into the first game against Silverwood College. They had nice smart shirts and a mini-bus that put ours to shame. Mind you, most of the mini-buses and coaches at the tournament put ours to shame. We didn't even have matching shorts, and I could hear the giggles from some of the other teams as we walked out onto the pitch.

A short time later the giggling had stopped. Silverwood were a nice bunch of girls, too nice. They were here to have some fun and not at all bothered about winning and it showed. We did want to win. Two goals from Leila and a great strike from Poppy had the game won before half-time. I managed to get onto the score sheet along with Zara for a 5-0 win. Ceder Valley, the other team in our mini group also beat them, 6-0. So, the final group match was simple. We needed to win. If it was a draw Ceder Valley would go through having scored more goals than us.

We kicked off that last group match full of determination but found that the Ceder's goalkeeper was really good. Twice I thought I had scored the opening goal, only to see her claw it away at the last moment. Poppy hit the post at the start of the second half when really she should have scored. But, we were dominating the game.

We were pushing harder and harder as the game wore on, but Ceder Valley refused to buckle. Time and time again our attacks were stopped. It began to look like we were going to be knocked out, having not lost a game, or conceded a goal. On one of the few counter attacks they had, Charley crunched into their striker and hurt herself in the process. Whilst she was down, we had a quick team talk with Rachel.

'Ok girls, this is it,' she said. 'This is what we need to do. Poppy, I want you to go wide, Leila, you go the other side and pull their defenders away from the centre. Izzy, Sophia, whoever gets the chance, I want you to drive through the middle, find that space. Let's win this game.'

Leila wasn't impressed.

'I'm the best striker we have,' I heard her say. 'I should be the one to score the goals.'

'Leila,' Rachel said, 'sometimes you need to do something no one expects. Ceder Valley expects you to be the one to score the goals, so their defenders will follow you everywhere. You can get an assist without even touching the ball.'

Leila was not happy, but as we entered the last few minutes, she looked at Poppy and they both span wide. The defenders who were marking them looked confused, hesitating before following them wide. Robyn had possession of the ball and hit a great pass from midfield, straight down the middle. The defenders saw what was happening, but it was too late. I had the space and the time as my speed had got me to the ball ahead of Sophia and their last defender. The keeper wanted to come out but hesitated and that was all the encouragement I needed as I fired the ball low and hard towards the corner. It scorched into the back of the net to the delight of my teammates who all screamed with delight.

Ceder Valley had no time to respond, and the referee blew her whistle to end their hopes but sent us into the next round of eliminators. Rachel was over the moon. She kept telling us how proud she was and how well we had done, that we weren't expected to get this far as it was the first time Falcon Hill had ever entered the National Championships.

'Girls, she said, 'I am so proud of you. You never stopped trying and even when you weren't sure about some of the instructions, you did it anyway. That's teamwork! Leila, Poppy, you get a huge assist for that last goal.' Leila flicked her long hair in a defiant gesture.

'I will still keep scoring the goals, Miss,' she said as she left the room with a smile on her face.

'I know you will,' Rachel said smiling.

Stonebridge Grammar School were another little school who always punched well above their weight. They had entered the National Championships every year for the past ten years and made the final stages on each occasion. Like us they came from a rugby playing mixed school and their girls, like us, had fought hard to earn their right to represent their school at football.

We were on the same path as they were, only many years behind. We were all determined to change that quickly and to prove to Blackthorpe that we should have the same chances as his beloved rugby boys.

We kicked off our first knockout game full of hope and enthusiasm, and we had every right to. Zara and Poppy ran the show once again. The Stonebridge girls didn't know how to cope with them, especially Zara. She was in a particularly mean mood having discovered that her parents weren't able to come home for her birthday.

She confided in me just before the game when I saw her face flushed with anger and tears in her eyes.

'They didn't even call me, Iz,' she said. 'They told me in a text message, I hate them!' she raged.

Her fury continued onto the pitch as she smashed into tackles and ran like a girl possessed by a demon. Rachel called to her to calm down several times, but through all the rage she was dominating her opponents. The game was reaching half-time, still somehow nil-nil, when Zara burst through knocking one poor Stonebridge girl flying. Into the penalty area and just as she was about to strike the ball, she felt a tap on her heel. A defender in a desperate attempt to stop her had tripped her and down she went, tumbling head over heels.

Penalty!

Zara didn't like that one little bit and turned round to grab the other girl. We had to pull her away as her anger threatened to boil over once again. I knew what had happened with her parents and understood now why she reacted the way she did, but it was going to be a real problem as the other team knew she could be wound up and would most likely get herself sent off. Rachel had recognised this, and as we watched Robyn casually stroke the penalty into the corner of the net for 1-0, Zara was being replaced by Tess.

It was amazing the effect her substitution had. Tess was a nice girl, but she wasn't a footballer to match Zara and found herself caught out several times, handing the girls from Stonebridge chance after chance. Maya who had little to do in the first half was called into action repeatedly, but when she was finally beaten, Charley was on hand and slid in to clear the ball off the line. We began to move the ball better, towards the end, and I was desperately guiding Tess through the game: where to stand, when to push up, when to drop off. It was hard, but I knew that we would need her, today and maybe later, in the tournament. All the information I had been given by Rachel was coming out; now I was the teacher! As the game reached its conclusion, Stonebridge was pushing hard for the equaliser. They were shocked at still being behind to a scruffy bunch of girls who they had expected to beat comfortably, such was our reputation – or lack of it.

They increased the pressure. A cross shot by their wiry winger should have been dealt with, but Charley for once hesitating, the Stonebridge striker pounced, producing a fierce shot past Maya's dive. I threw myself towards the ball only to feel a searing pain as the ball cannoned into my stomach before flying up high into the air. The ball looped and swirled as it fell, and we all watched in hope and desperation as it clipped the crossbar and went behind.

There was no time for Stonebridge to take the corner and the referee blew her whistle. That was it. All over. I was horribly winded and struggled to join in with the celebrations. The Stonebridge girls were on their knees, shattered and devastated at having lost, after playing so well in that second half. As the pain in my stomach reduced, it was replaced by a massive sense of pride and satisfaction. We had taken Falcon Hill to the knockout stages of the National Cup and were now amongst the best teams in the whole country. The first time a team from our school, boys or girls, had gone this far.

Surely now Blackthorpe would take note of us?

The journey home was fun. Winning always helps, but I had Zara on my mind. I spoke to Miss Hunter and between us we persuaded the driver to pull over in a shopping centre, we all piled out. Still in our grubby football kit, we raided the shops for presents for Zara. We got back on the bus singing happy birthday to Zara on repeat! I'd even managed to find a card and a birthday cake. The card said 'Happy 21st Birthday,' but Zara just laughed and put the badge on anyway. It was good to see her smiling, sitting there with her red and blue hair poking out from under a new hat I had found in the bargain bucket section of one of the shops.

'I don't care what it cost, Iz,' she said. 'It's a great present, thank you.' Zara seemed to carry sadness around with her. I knew she didn't really 'hate' her parents, but she missed them terribly. I just couldn't understand why they paid her so little attention. It made me incredibly grateful that I had both my parents supporting me. I was truly lucky.

By the time we got home, we all felt a bit car-sick. Pizza, milkshake and cake, plus a bumpy bus ride didn't help. Zara ended up sleeping over on the couch in my room. She had more rooms in her house than you could count, yet here she was, just wanting to be around a family. She sat quietly, with a big smile on her face at breakfast the next morning. Dad had made his famed 'dad's breakie.' Bacon and eggs in a roll, but he did something with the eggs and the roll that made it taste incredible. Zara loved it, asking for a second helping and laughing even more as we watched Jack's egg dribble down his chin.

Reputation is what people think of you. Character is what you are.

We went into the school assembly the next morning full of pride at our achievements, fully expecting a hero's welcome from the school staff and indeed, stubborn old Blackthorpe.

He babbled on about lessons, and discipline. Talked about a student who had won a science competition. Another who had written a short story that was going into the local newspaper. It was, as usual, a painful experience.

'And now to our sports teams,' he proudly announced, before recounting the boy's rugby game almost in its entirety. They had won so he was rightly pleased, but surely we were next? Clearly not.

He was just about to wrap up his rugby monologue when I glanced over towards Miss Hunter. She was fuming, her face flushed red with anger. Blackthorpe must have sensed it as he glanced over to her.

'Oh yes, the girls,' he said, looking away from Miss Hunters' death stare whilst he pretended to shuffle some papers. 'I nearly forgot. The girls' football team won their game too. Well done, now off you go to class and have a good day.'

'Was that it?' Robyn was standing in the doorway blocking everyone from escaping to their lessons. Charley was equally annoyed.

'We reach the knockout stages of the national cup, the best 16 schools in the country and that's all we get. A 'well done' one-liner?' she said.

Tayla and I just stood open mouthed.

'I don't get it, was he not proud?' I said.

'If it was the boys, they would have their names engraved on the wall,' joked Poppy.

School dragged that day, for all of us. By the time I got home, I was quite deflated and collapsed in a heap in the corner of my room.

'Izzy, are you ok?' mum had found me hiding in my room amongst a pile of Accies football shirts and scarves that Jack and I had collected over the years. I told her about the assembly and about how let down I felt.

'It's not just me mum, it's the others. It's Miss Hunter too. She was so angry'.

'I can imagine,' mum replied. 'But it's not about him, or the other teachers, or even the other teams. You and your friends are on a journey now. A really exciting one. Dad and I know how hard you have all worked. Jack was telling his coach all about your game this morning, and how you saved the day with your late block.'

I instinctively reached for my sore ribs and stomach, where a ball shaped bruise had coloured my skin different shades of red, black and yellow.

'I know Mum,' I said, wincing as I pressed on the bruised area. 'But it would have been nice to have been mentioned in the assembly. We are representing the school after all.'

The next day before training, Rachel sat us all down for a chat.

'Ok girls,' she said. 'I know you are all disappointed with the headmaster about his lack of enthusiasm regarding girls' football. I had words with him afterward and he knows how cross I was with his lack of support. But the fact is, we are in the knockout stages of the

National Cup, and this is our chance to shine as a team. We, in this room, need to stick together. Our little band here is all that matters. I am behind you 100%,' she smiled.

We went out for training and worked our socks off. Once again, I stayed behind with Poppy and Zara to practice a bit more. Poppy wanted to practice her free kicks and corners. Zara just didn't want to go home! We stayed until it was dark. Practicing routines, chatting and working out tactics. I walked past Tayla's house on the way to see Sophia, and as promised gave her a hand with some of her chores. I knew that without her energy in the midfield, Zara and I wouldn't have the space to be able to play. If we could help her, even a little, we would.

This pattern continued for the next couple of weeks as we prepared for the next game. We had seen the draw for the next few rounds and could plan the route and who we might be up against all the way to the final. The good news was that Millbrook House was on the opposite side of the draw, so we would avoid the purple and golds unless we both reached the final. Probable for them. Unlikely for us! Word began to get around that I was staying longer and later than everyone else to practice with anyone who fancied it and bit by bit, more and more players joined in to practice, whether it was shooting, passing, talking tactics or just having fun as a group of friends. The day before our last 16 match we had a team meeting. Sophia stood up before anyone could speak.

'Ok,' she announced, 'we all know how important the game is tomorrow, so it has to be perfect on and off the pitch. I love this team, and I love being the captain, but I think we all know who the glue is holding this team together. Izzy, you have helped me so much on and off the field in the last few weeks, I wouldn't be able to play without you, so with Miss Hunters' permission I want you to have this.'

She stepped forward and handed me her captain's armband.

'Don't think I won't still shout at you if you are in the wrong place though,' she said with a smile. Everyone else held their breath for a second, at first not quite realising what was going on, then they began to clap in appreciation of both the gesture from Sophia and recognising that I had become such an important part of this team.

I opened my mouth, but no words came out.

Eventually, my voice cracking with emotion, I managed a

'Thank you. I promise I won't let you down.'

'We know you won't,' said Rachel. 'You never do!'

Nothing beats stepping on the pitch and proving the doubters wrong.

The tournament had reached the last 16 schools. 15 of the 16 remaining entrants had been here before. We were the only ones who hadn't, but I knew we had a great chance of going further.

We had individual talent that was slowly being harnessed into an exciting team. When we attacked, we could be breathtaking. We had skill and speed and were all willing to help each other.

Our next opponents, Lakeside International School, was filled with overseas students who had come to spend time in the UK to learn English. They came from all over the world. From the Americas, across Europe, India, and

China. They had lots of girls who could play, but their problem was communication with each other. With English as their second language, they often struggled, but they had girls with real talent. It was a tough draw.

Rachel decided to drop Robyn into defence and move Poppy back into midfield, to give more protection to Maya in goal. She had seen the previous game Lakeside had played and realised how good their strikers were. We would have to battle hard to keep them out.

Letting them score a goal in the first five minutes was not part of the plan. A silly mistake by me allowed Lakeside to regain possession, and as the cross was fired across the box their striker slid in unmarked to turn it past a flatfooted Maya.

My first game as captain and we were losing so early. We struggled to get into the game, and even packing our midfield we couldn't get the game under control. I found myself getting pushed deeper and deeper and as the shots rained in on our goal it was surely only a matter of time before they killed us off. But we hung on. Charley and Tayla at the heart of our defence were immense and we battled for every ball.

Half time came, and with it a chance to

reset. Zara pulled me to one side.

'Iz, you can't do it all,' she said. 'You need to trust us to do our job, and you need to push on. Use your speed, push them back.'

She was right. We had hardly tested them in the first half. Leila was a spectator for much of it, hoping to get a half chance, to feed off any scraps left by an increasingly confident Lakeside defence.

As soon as the whistle went to resume the game, I turned on the afterburners. For the next 10 minutes I didn't run, I motored! Sprinting to everything, letting my first touch do the job I had been practicing for, for months. The Lakeside players realised what a threat I was, but didn't know how to handle me. Two of their players were drawn to me as they knew I was too fast to catch if I managed to get away. What this allowed, though, was space for my teammates, which Zara and Poppy then exploited wonderfully well.

Receiving the ball with my back to their goal, I flicked it sideways under pressure from my double markers. Zara received my pass before she glided past a couple of half-hearted challenges, setting up a great chance for Poppy. She controlled the ball on the edge of the box before drilling it hard and low. The

Lakeside keeper made a good attempt but there was too much pace on the ball, and it zipped into the net for the equaliser. We pushed on, Zara and I again combining well deep in our own half. A quick pass released Poppy down the wing, who found herself playing provider this time, as her long deep cross found Leila sliding in at the far post to make it 2-1.

Lakeside's heads were down. They knew they should have taken their chances in the first half and were now staring at defeat. My markers had lost their discipline and had begun to look over at Poppy, Zara and the enthusiastic Robyn. But even then, I still had lots of work to do as I collected a loose ball on the halfway line. I pushed the ball past the nearest defender and accelerated away. Even when I raced my brother Jack at home, he always commented that my ability to accelerate from a standing start made me tough to catch. Even when hitting top speed, he was always behind me over those first few crucial metres. The Lakeside girls were nowhere near as quick as Jack, and I was able to race down the wing. We had all worked so hard up until that point that none of my teammates were able to respond. Leila, having chased shadows in the first half, was exhausted, so I went it alone. Cutting inside I ghosted past another defender, nutmegging another before clipping the ball over the goalkeeper as she rushed towards me. There was a stunned hesitation on the touchline as the ball hit the back of the net before our supporters erupted. I screamed with delight. Captain for the first time, and surely now into the quarter-finals of the cup.

There were only a few minutes left, but Lakeside had given up and we just went through the motions before the referee ended the match. The Lakeside girls all came to shake my hand and congratulate me on my goal as well as our win. They all said they hoped we went on to win the cup.

It was something I hadn't really thought about. We had wanted to do well, to represent our school and to make Mr Blackthorpe sit up and take notice. But none of us expected to get to this stage.

'Congratulations, Miss Harvey,' came a deep voice.

I turned round sharply, flushing red with embarrassment. I had no idea who the man was, but I was in no doubt where he was from, with his purple blazer with gold writing carefully hand-sewn initials 'MBH School' and a pair of incredibly shiny shoes.

'Thank you,' I smiled.

The man carried on,

'A quite brilliant goal, and an all-round great performance. A true captain's performance. We like that sort of attitude where I am from. Maybe one day you might like to wear a blazer like this one?'

My jaw dropped, mouth wide open in astonishment. Before I could muster a response, I saw Rachel looking over quizzically.

'Isabelle?' she called.

'Gotta go, bye,' I said to the man as I ran off towards my team.

'What was that all about?' Tayla had seen the chat I had just had and wanted to know all about it. 'That stuffed shirt, why was he here?' she continued.

Robyn was next to her, and she knew why he was there too.

'I think they have heard all about the mighty Falcons and are scared,' she said, and we both laughed. Although it was something I thought about for the rest of the day. Why was someone from Millbrook House watching our game? My mind was racing for the rest of the day. If he had come to watch the team, why had he come over to speak to me and me alone? Jack was equally confused.

'Why was he there?' he asked. 'Millbrook House had their own knockout game to prepare for. I reckon he was one of their scouts. They look to take the best players and put them in their academy. The Accies ladies' team would probably take you now if they saw you play!' he said.

'That's my dream too,' I said. But the Accies ladies' team is an amateur team. I would have to get a job too. The MBH academy pays for everything, don't they?'

'I think you are getting a bit ahead of yourself Izzy,' Mum had come in. 'He just came over to speak to you. Maybe it was just that he was impressed by your goal. We all were!'

It was a broken night's sleep for me. I kept whirling the idea of the MBH academy in my head. The Accies Academy had been my goal, my dream. They were my dads' team. My brother was going to be the next superstar there, I was sure of that. But I had always thought I would end up playing there too. Maybe now there was another option, I mean, imagine going to school at the famous

Millbrook House. Playing football on those incredible pitches. In their Academy being watched by scouts from all of the big professional teams every week.

I sat in my English lesson, paying next to no interest to the teacher as she explained something about the Shakespeare play we were about to read. My head was swimming and as I whispered to Tayla, she began to get excited too.

'He must have been there for a reason, Izzy,' she said. 'Even if it wasn't to see you, he would have been impressed. You were brilliant the whole match.'

'Thanks,' I replied, 'but I've only ever wanted to play for the Accies, what do I do if they ask me?'

Tayla laughed and caught a glare from the teacher.

'I think you'd best wait until they ask you first. Anyway, you don't need to worry about that just yet! We've got a cup quarter-final to get ready for.'

The sky belongs to those who dare to rise. Play with passion, fight with all of your heart. Show them what someone with a crazy dream can do.

The quarter-final would be a tough fixture. We were to travel away to one of the big comprehensive schools up in the north of England. They had a reputation of being tough competitors and despite it being spring, the weather did not look favourable. The rain that week came down day and night and we were left to train in the school hall, not ideal preparation.

We set out on the coach early on that Friday morning. It was a long drive there, at least six hours sitting not being able to move. We could only stare out the window at the black clouds as the rain continued to hammer down, watching as the coach splashed through the puddles at the side of the road. What was in our favour was the school we were playing against, was in a town at the top of a hill. So, whilst everywhere was very wet, the game was definitely on. No phones or screens were allowed on the coach, so I sat and read, occasionally falling asleep. The closer we got, the noisier the bus got as the other girls began to get more and more excited about the game. We were one win away from a remarkable achievement, reaching the semi-finals. Being able to call ourselves one of the best four teams in the whole of the country.

It seemed like the whole of Orchard Lane Comprehensive School had turned out to support their girls. They had banners, horns and drums. There was a lot of shouting, a lot of colour. It was the best atmosphere I had ever played in.

As we ran out it truly felt like we were the enemy.

Orchard Lane kicked off and immediately we realised how hard the game was going to be. The wind and the rain were in our faces, and they pushed hard to put us under pressure. Amara and Ava were tested at the back; Amara uncharacteristically was making a few mistakes and because of that we struggled to get out of our half.

It was no surprise that they scored first. Maya had already made a couple of decent saves, coming up dripping in mud each time as the pitch began to cut up. But even she was powerless to prevent their opening goal. A deep cross, driven in from the right-hand side and stroked into the bottom corner. We appeared to get a bit more of a foothold in the game as the half wore on, and despite the conditions, I managed to get my foot on the ball and began to play. But as a dark cloud loomed large over our heads, the gusty wind noticeably picked up and made every clearance, every pass forward a challenge. I picked the ball up in midfield and tried to switch the play to Sophie who was out wide, but the wind held the ball up and it was comfortably intercepted by the tall Orchard Lane central defender. She strode forward unchallenged, and just as Zara was about to close her down, she let fly with a thunderous drive. Maya was helpless, and her desperate dive had no effect as the ball scorched past her despairing clutches into the net for 2-0.

Rachel desperately tried to shout instructions from the halfway line, but amongst the banging of their drums and the wind we couldn't hear her. She had wanted us to tighten up, not chase the game so early on, and with the conditions so against us, but we wanted to get a goal back. We came close. My drive through the middle, and pass to the speedy Robyn, opened up the Orchard defence. She crossed high to the back post where both Zara and Poppy were, hungry for a goal and for us to get back into the game. As Zara jumped, she crashed into Poppy and the defender who was desperately trying to stay with them and could only watch as the ball sailed harmlessly over everyone's heads. Both Zara and Poppy were furious with each other and so busy arguing whose fault it was, that they were not paying attention as Orchard Lane counter-attacked.

The ball was fed down the line where Poppy should have been. The Orchard Lane girls outnumbered us and with some clever passing, they bore down on the overwhelmed Amara. She did her best, stretching to block the shot but as she did so she twisted awkwardly and fell. They simply rolled the ball sideways past her to a teammate who slipped it past Maya into the empty net for 3-0.

'That's it, all over,' I said to myself. Tears

were welling up inside me as we trudged back towards our changing room. All except Amara. She was squealing in pain as she was helped off the pitch by Rachel. Zara and Poppy were still arguing, Tayla kicked a drinking bottle so hard, the top split and showered the wall in water. Tess came in. She had been on the substitutes bench and was now taking her jacket off.

Miss Fletcher, who had been helping Rachel out with some of the coaching sessions, had come over to talk to us.

'Amara is off to hospital to get checked out,' she said calmly. There's nothing more we can do for her now. We just need to try and do something about this scoreline.' The calmness in her voice eased our concerns slightly, but not the sound of sirens as an ambulance took poor Amara away.

'We need to stop arguing with each other and play to the conditions,' I said. 'We have the wind behind us now. We know we can create chances. But we have to be patient. There is plenty of time left.'

'Izzy, it's 3-0. We're out. We've lost. What chance do we have?' Charley asked angrily.

'None, unless you believe it's possible. We owe it to Amara to go out and at least make this respectable. Get one goal back and then we will see what they are made of.'

There was silence as my teammates digested what I had said.

Zara stood up.

'Let's do this for Amara. Come on!' she cried, as we trooped back out into the wind and rain.

Credit to the Orchard Lane School, there was still a big crowd watching despite the awful weather. Winning a surprisingly one-sided half had helped. Their makeshift band of drums was hammering away as we kicked off the second half. This time we set about our game plan immediately. We had pushed Tess into the midfield, leaving only three defenders. It was a risk, but we figured if we could overwhelm them in midfield, we didn't need so many defenders. With the wind in our favour, that was the case, and we pushed them back time and again. From a corner, we got a goal back. A terrific header from Charley into the roof of the net with the Orchard Lane keeper rooted to her line.

'Now do you believe it?' I screamed with delight as we grabbed the ball and sprinted back into our half, ready to restart the game. Seconds later we were right back in the game. I won the ball in midfield with a crunching tackle, the ball squirting out sideways to Robyn who sped off down the wing. I had picked myself up and was sprinting at full speed to catch up. Robyn crossed the ball back to me and I hit it on the volley - first-time from outside of the penalty area. It would have been the goal of the season had it gone in, but it was not quite accurate enough. The keeper, however, could only parry the slippery ball. Sophia was alive and alert enough to have followed the flight of the ball, and as it rolled loose, she was the first one to the rebound and had the easiest job of rolling it into the unguarded net.

'One more!' I cried as again we scooped up the ball from their net and ran back to restart. Orchard Lane was looking visibly worried, and their crowd had quietened considerably, as once again we robbed them of possession and set about pushing them back. We were all over them, the extra midfielder was working. Leila and Poppy were getting chance after chance. Their keeper was doing her best but even she was powerless to prevent the flying Falcons.

Tess was having a surprisingly good game having joined the battle. Picking up a loose ball after another crunching tackle - this time from

Tayla - she set us on our way once again. Passing neatly to Robyn, who moved the ball onto Sophia. I had seen the space in behind and motored away. Sophia saw me and chipped the ball into the space, the bouncing ball sat up perfectly for me. I had seen the keeper was caught on the edge of her area, too far away to close me down, but too far away from her goal. I smashed the ball hard towards the target. As soon as I made the connection, I just knew I had caught it well. The ball flew off the sweet spot of my foot, arching with power and pace over their keeper who just watched as the net bulged for a third time.

3-3. We had done it. We had turned it around, but we weren't finished.

We strode forward with the wind at our backs. Orchard Lane didn't know how to handle us. Zara and Robyn were ripping their midfield to pieces, and I was leading by example with my passing which was spot on, even in the wet tricky conditions. Time after time we closed in on what we thought would be the winning goal, but it just would not go in. The only respite Orchard Lane got was when we missed the target and they had a goal kick, enabling them to clear briefly.

The Orchard supporters to their credit had

stuck with their team. They realised that we were all playing the conditions as much as we were playing each other, and they tried to rally their team with a big round of drum playing. Boom, boom, boom! The deep vibration of the drums echoed through us, and it seemed to get louder as - for once - they managed to get through the tigerish tackling of our midfielders. They had made a few changes, and some fresh legs had come on, including one particularly tall girl who made me look very short indeed. She was very skilful and Charley was unable to get the ball off her; as she turned and shot, the ball flicked off Charley's boot and spun goalwards in the opposite direction to Maya's dive. We all watched helplessly as the ball curved and spun on the wet grass, nestling into the corner of our net: 3-4.

We had only minutes remaining and my teammates looked crestfallen. We had all worked so hard and it looked like we were done for.

I knew it was up to me to lift the team and as soon as Poppy kicked off, I demanded the ball. The Orchard girls knew I was fast, and they were standing away from me, trying to work out what to do as I drove forward. I beat one player, then a second; swerving left, then right. A defender finally moved in to challenge me, but using one of my brothers' tricks, I rolled my foot over the ball one way before pushing it the other way through the legs of the defender, hurdling her as she slipped and fell. I was through. No one had the speed to get close to me, Leila Poppy and Zara were all desperately trying to catch up, but I was away and bearing down on the goal. The keeper, knowing I had a powerful shot, refused to close me down for fear of being chipped again, but this played into my hands as she left a big gap at the far corner. I looked down and struck the ball with the inside of my foot, the ball curling across the face of the goal, striking the inside of the post before rebounding back into the net on the other side.

'GOAAAAAAAAAAAL!' I screamed, running off in circles, not quite knowing who to run to. It was without doubt the best goal I'd ever scored, except perhaps for the back-heeled volley I had made against Jack's mate Lucas, messing about in our back garden.

'WE - DO - NOT - LET - THIS - GO,' I demanded, as the girls surrounded me in a jubilant huddle. 'We finish this now,' I shouted above the noise. 'We don't want extra time: one more goal.'

The exhausted Orchard girls had decided that extra time was their target now and sat back, defending as best they could. There must have been only seconds remaining when my cross-shot clipped a defender's heels and went behind for a corner. Zara had shown her accuracy with the ball even in these conditions, so it was obvious who we wanted to take the corner. Orchard Lane expected another one of her high swirling crosses that had been causing them all kinds of trouble up till now, so they were surprised by her low drilled cross, zipping across the wet grass. It caused all kinds of mayhem: miskicks, half-cleared swipes, scuffed shots, the ball bobbled about. The referee had already looked at her watch several times before the corner and I was sure that this was our last chance to win it. Sophia at last had a clean shot, which was well-saved down low by the keeper. It was going out for another corner when I stretched and dragged it back into play. Their desperate keeper was up quickly and had tried to pounce on the ball, but as I pulled the ball back from the goal line, she couldn't stop her momentum and crashed into me, sending me sprawling. The shrill whistle of the referee rang through my ears, cutting sharply through the noise of the crowd. Time seemed to pause as we all froze mid-motion, breaths held and eyes darting to see what the call would be.

'Penalty,' she cried.

I had already grabbed the ball, offering it first to Leila, then Poppy, then Sophia, all of which shook their head. Even Robyn turned it down.

'No Iz,' she said as I begged her to take the ball. 'This is your moment. You've pulled us back from the edge, and now you can finish the job,' she said smiling as she pushed the ball back towards me.

The drums had stopped. The crowd had a deathly hush as I placed the ball onto the muddy penalty spot. I closed my eyes. 'What would Jack do? What would Dad say?' I thought. The referee blew her whistle. I opened my eyes again and took several deep breaths before approaching the ball. The keeper swayed left, then right before diving left just as I struck the ball, hard, high, and straight. It rocketed into the goal sending a fine spray of water droplets high into the sky as the net rippled for my hattrick. I hardly had a chance to take a breath before my teammates bowled me to the ground in an ecstatic celebration. We had made the semi-finals! Amongst the mayhem, the referee blew the final whistle, confirming our passage was secure.

If you do what you've always done, you will get what you've always got. Don't fear change. Embrace the unknown.

The next few days I felt I was on cloud nine. My hattrick was all anyone could talk about, and even grumpy Blackthorpe gave me a mention in the school assembly, even if it was a side note after we had heard everything about his boys' exploits.

We were more worried about poor Amara and what was happening to her. She missed the whole week at school and when she came back, her foot was in a giant boot and she was on crutches. She told us that her ankle was broken, and she needed to have an operation. It would be in the next few days, and it would mean she would not be allowed to do any sport at all for a long time, let alone play football.

Miss Hunter sat us all down, with Amara, and they both spoke about how proud they were of our result in the quarter finals. Amara was tearful, but she held herself well, although we could see how sad she was. I was determined that we would make the final for her. And that week as we trained, I could see that everyone else had the same view. There was an edge about us. Fully focused.

Although some of the tackling threatened to get out of hand, Rachel had to remind us occasionally that we were all on the same side! I spent a lot of time that next week with Tayla and Zara. We had come to know Zara well, and whilst she still dressed like a rebel and now had red, blue and yellow streaks in her hair, much to the disgust of Blackthorpe, she had settled down in the classroom, not giving any of the teacher's chance to reprimand her.

After lessons, we were glued to our screens watching every clip we could find of our next opponents, Newlands Academy. A big school with a huge catchment area. They had a lot more girls to choose from than we did. Over treble in fact. They always put out decent teams and had good runs in the National

Championship. They had reached the semi-finals last year and had won the tournament a few years ago. They looked really good, but we felt we had an edge in midfield.

With me and Sophia either side of Tess, and Zara and Robyn backing us up, we knew we could dominate the midfield. As the lower ranked school, we had to travel once again. It seemed a bit unfair that we were up against the opposition supporters once again, but there was nothing we could do about it.

The early morning sun crept over the field, casting long shadows across the freshly cut grass. Crowds of parents, friends, and a few curious onlookers were gathering on the sidelines. Everyone was buzzing with excitement as they found their places in the stand or at the side of the pitch.

Newlands were brimming with talent. Many of their girls were on the books of professional academies. We were filled with excitement and nerves. I stood at the front of the line, holding my head high. I kept glancing over my shoulder to make sure everyone looked ready. We needed to show them that we belonged here, even if we might have felt like we were second best.

'This is it,' I said, 'we've worked so hard all

season for this chance. No one expected us to get this far. Let's play for each other, stay focused, and let's show them what we can do!'

Newlands would be tough competitors. Known for their attacking style and skilful strikers, they had a reputation that left most teams they played feeling intimidated. But not me, not today. I was still feeling on top of the world after my player-of-the-match performance in the quarter-final. I also was very aware that there would be a lot of scouts watching today. We had some of the best schoolgirl footballers in the country playing, and I was determined to be one of them and put on a good show for them.

Newlands' towering captain approached the centre circle as I stood with the referee. She flashed a smile in my direction. She looked confident, safe in the knowledge that she had already been snapped up by the Northdale United Academy, one of the biggest and best clubs in the country. It felt like she knew that the result would already be going in their favour when she looked at me. I could see it in her eyes, how could these scruffy-looking girls even create a chance against us? It made me even more focused as I shook her hand.

From the first whistle, they went on the

attack, moving down the field with quick, confident passes. Our defence was in action immediately, Charley and Ava both conceding corners in the first couple of minutes after last-ditch tackles saved what had looked like good scoring opportunities. We were pushed further and further back, both Robyn and I dropping into defensive positions. We were fortunate that Maya chose today to be at her most agile best; all those dance lessons and gymnastic competitions came to good use as she flung herself about her area making save after save.

The crowd was again very noisy, it was something we were getting used to, but at least this time we had some fans of our own to cheer us on. Jack and the Accies Academy boys had been playing in a league game down the road the night before, and he had convinced the whole squad to come down and support his little sister. They were all getting very involved, cheering every pass and tackle we made. I had to admit, they all looked the part in matching ties and blazers - All paid for by the club of course. Their philosophy was: if you look good, and feel good, then your performance will be better as a result.

Play continued at a relentless pace. Midway through the first half, Zara intercepted a pass and drove down the field with speed. She dribbled past one defender, then another, her feet almost a blur. Sensing her opportunity, she fired a shot toward the goal from the edge of the box. The ball sailed through the air, only to be deflected by the Newlands keeper's outstretched hand. The crowd gasped as it flew goalwards and then cheered what was an incredible save.

It was a close call and one of the few chances we created in that first half. But we weren't disheartened. And as half time arrived - still scoreless - I could feel the energy in the team rising.

Rachel made some tweaks to the formation. Robyn and I - as probably the fittest and fastest players in the team - were moved to wing-back positions. Zara and Sophia would protect Tess in the middle, and it was left to Poppy and Leila to do the damage up front.

As the second half began, the game grew more physical. The Newlands players were tackling harder, and every 50-50 was contested with intensity. Zara was shoved off the ball, landing with a thud. But as the referee's whistle echoed across the field for a free kick she reacted angrily, shoving the Newlands player. I sprinted over to pull her away but as I did, I accidentally crashed into another Newlands player, and we all went flying. The referee called us all over and we got an angry dressing down. All four of us received a yellow card, but I was held for longer. Even though it was entirely accidental, the referee didn't see it that way.

'You are the captain of this team,' she said sternly. 'You need to set an example. I can't have you charging over every time there is an incident you don't like. I am the one who deals with that, not you.'

I felt my face going bright red with embarrassment and as the game kicked off again, I was hesitant, which meant I missed a simple opportunity to win the ball back, leading to a great Newlands chance. The ball fizzed across the box to the tall Newlands captain who met the ball perfectly. Maya got her arm to the ball but couldn't stop it. It squirmed underneath her, but fortunately for us Tayla – at full stretch – was able to hack the ball off the line and keep the game nil-nil.

The more chances they missed, the more I believed we were going to do it. We had worked tirelessly the whole game. We had stuck to Rachel's game plan and time and again, the Newlands girls were frustrated. If we were honest, they were the better team, but I knew we had bigger hearts.

We had gone on this amazing journey, where nobody had given us a chance. Even our headmaster had told us he hadn't even expected us to get out of our preliminary group, and here we were, half a game away from a place in the final. Some of these girls hadn't played a proper game of football before this season, but as a group of friends, we had come together over the course of our run in the competition, and there surely was no team at any level who were as tight a group as we were.

As the game wore on, I couldn't help but notice a section of the crowd wasn't joining in with the noise. They were all in their purple and gold blazers. It was the Millbrook House girl's squad. They were here to see who they were going to play in the final. They had won their semi-final - emphatically 4-0 - and had travelled over to watch our game, looking for weaknesses no doubt.

'Well, they won't find any from me,' I thought. I allowed myself a moment to let my mind wander. What it would be like to represent Millbrook House, wear that gleaming purple and gold uniform. Walking in through those giant front gates. Playing football on that beautiful carpet-like football pitch. Have my name on my personalised locker in the changing rooms, with all my achievements listed underneath.

I quickly snapped out of my daydream, I had a duty to Falcon Hill and the girls as their captain.

I drove the team on, shouting encouragement when we didn't have the ball, and barking instructions when we did. I passed and tackled like it was the World Cup final, and gradually I began to notice that the Newlands defenders were getting tired. At a break in play, I stood next to Zara.

'Look Za, they are exhausted,' I said.

'So am I Izzy,' Zara laughed. 'You've run us into the ground as well as them,' she said smiling.

'Ok, sorry,' I replied, 'but I still feel good. Get the ball to me, anyway you can.'

She nodded and ran off, passing the message to the others as she went back to her position. Newlands still were a danger and a deep cross to the back post looked worrying, until Maya reached her long lean arms into the sky and plucked the ball out of the air. She bowled the ball out to Ava, who quickly moved it onto Tess. She didn't hang onto the ball for long as it went wide to Robyn. Rather than beat her marker for pace, she simply laid the ball inside to Sophia and received it back after she had moved forward. Again, she quickly whipped the ball in towards Poppy who knew I was steaming up to support her. She rolled the ball forward into my path and with one touch I was away once again, this time in a pure 50-50 with the goalkeeper. I rarely lost a race, against girls or boys of my age, and I reached the ball before my opponent did. The angle I was running was not a good one and I quickly realised if I tried to go around her, I would be heading away from the goal, so I tried a little chip. It worked perfectly as the keeper desperately tried to make herself as big as possible by spreading her arms and legs in a star shape, but the ball went over her shoulder and into the net. 1-0.

We erupted in celebration. The Accies boys were bouncing about at the side of the pitch like a bunch of lunatics. I could hear Jack shouting at the top of his lungs: 'That's my sister, that's my sister!'

But with fifteen minutes left, we knew they would come back at us. No one was sitting now, every parent, student or supporter on the sidelines were standing, hands clutched nervously. Wave after wave of shots and crosses rained down upon us. Charley was having a brilliant game once again. She won every challenge. Her training as a rugby player was coming to good use, as no one could push her about. I was playing almost as a central defender now and we left just Leila up front to chase any desperate clearances that came her way.

With less than a minute to go, Newlands made one last push. Their captain sprinted down the sideline, for once breaking past the tiring Robyn. She played a clever 1-2 with another girl before crossing over my head to the far post. The ball was brought down by a Newlands striker who dropped her shoulder, finally beating the despairing lunge of Charley before firing a fierce shot toward the corner of the goal. The ball clipped my heel, but the ball was still fizzing towards the corner of the net. Maya threw herself, her fingers just grazing the ball as it curved slightly. We held our breath. It missed the goalpost by a millimetre, skidding out of danger and off the pitch.

The corner was fired in with pace, it pinged around the box with no one able to clear it or shoot effectively, but we somehow managed to get rid of it and as it fell to Tayla, she thumped it as hard as she could towards the touchline, much to the obvious disappointment of the majority of the Newlands crowd. The final whistle blew, and for a split second, the field went silent. Then, cheers erupted from the Falcons' supporters as we celebrated our hard-fought victory. We had done it.

Against all the odds we were heading to the final.

As we walked off the field, exhausted but exhilarated, I glanced back at the pitch.

'Your journey isn't over yet,' came a voice.

It was the Newlands' captain. 'You have to win the final now,' she said. 'That was a brilliant performance. We had all heard about this amazing midfield superhero from Falcon Hill, but nobody realised quite how good you were.'

'Thanks,' I blushed.

'Enjoy this,' she said. 'Now go and win the final. We will see you next season ok,' she smiled.

One more game, I thought. This school had never been in a national final before, boys or girls, at any sport. We had never even been close. One more win, and we'd make history.

But for now, we would savour this victory, our sights set firmly on the final.

Don't let the fears in your mind push you about. Be led by the dreams in your heart. If you don't have a dream, how can you make your dreams come true?

If my school friends were happy for us before, now we were treated like royalty. We were even asked to come up to the stage during the Monday morning assembly. Blackthorpe told the school how proud he was of us all, and that he always knew we would do well. I glanced at Zara who fake yawned and rolled her eyes. A group at the front of the audience saw this and giggled, which drew an annoyed glare from the headmaster.

Rachel sat proudly off to the side. She had refused to come up to the stage with us.

'This is your time girls,' she said. 'I've had my moments. Now it's your chance to shine.

Your time to take the applause from the school for once.'

Blackthorpe hadn't finished. He had waffled on about who had done what, when and how for about 10 minutes. We had all pretty much switched off and not paying attention when he stated;

'Oh, and one last thing.'

We all turned to look at him as he rummaged in a box.

'If these girls are to represent this school in a national final, we can't have them wearing an old tatty kit with socks that don't match.' He continued, 'I have had these made up for you all' he said pulling out a yellow and blue shirt with the image of a Falcon on the crest, the symbol of our school. 'Fly high girls,' he said, as we all stood shocked and delighted at the same time. 'You've come this far, now go and win the thing!'

We had two weeks until the final. We found out that the game would actually be played at Millbrook House school. It was the best pitch available and could cope with lots of people. They were expecting a big crowd. It was a final after all. We thought it was a bit unfair that we were playing on the opposition's home pitch, but I didn't mind too much. The surface was perfect, and I loved the walk through the arches, down the long corridors filled with famous sports-stars, all of which attended this prestigious school. Everything about the school screamed excellence, and I knew only the very best or the cleverest girls received a scholarship there.

We became celebrities in our town. As captain, I was interviewed for the local news. Our scruffy team photo was even put in an online football magazine that covered local football at every level, all the way up to the professional sides. Even though Millbrook House was only a few miles away from Falcon Hill, the locals only seemed to want to talk about us.

We were massive underdogs and people seemed to like that. No one had given us a chance. Some of our players hadn't even played a proper game before this season. But we had worked hard, supported each other, and were helped by having some really good players backed by our brilliant coach. There was no doubt in my mind that no matter how hard we had wanted this, without Miss Hunter's help and guidance, we would have been beaten a long time ago.

The week of the final, the local paper put a

double page spread on the school team, headlining it, 'The Rise of the Falcons.' I loved it, it helped that there was a great action shot of me (and Zara as a former Millbrook student). It had pride of place next to a picture of the England Lionesses Euro winning side. The next page only had a small section on Millbrook House. They had won this tournament before and would always be in the mix every season because of the way they recruited the best girls from across the country. But the main focus and popular interest was on the 'Soaring Falcons.'

Blackthorpe had even invited a local news crew to watch one of our training sessions. Rachel wasn't best impressed as she was tripping over wires, and we were having to run round the camera crew when we should have been focussed on practicing the drills she had designed specifically for the final. But we still had a smile on our faces. It was so exciting.

On the eve of the match Rachel called us all in for a team meeting. Amara was there too. She had been for her operation which was a success. We were all devastated to have lost her on the pitch, but it was great to see her and have her around. She was doing her best to be happy for us, but I could see she was so sad at having been forced to miss out.

'This is obviously an important match,' Miss Hunter said, 'but don't forget, it's just another game of football. Whatever happens I am so proud of you for getting this far and you must be proud of yourselves. Let's not be intimidated by the opposition. They were watching our last game. They know what we can do and are capable of. They will be worried about us too. Go home, rest and I will see you all tomorrow.'

I knew I wouldn't be able to sit still, or concentrate that evening, so I pestered my dad into taking a few of us to go and watch Jack play for the Accies under 18's. The game was on the Accies' senior teams training pitch, which was set across the road in the shadows of the big main stand of the mighty Accies stadium. The glory days when the biggest and best teams from across Europe came, (and usually lost,) may have gone for now, but I was sure that my brother Jack was not just going to get into the team but be their new superstar. I was hoping that I could do the same. I had heard a rumour that Zara and Robyn had both been spoken to already by some of the Accies scouts about signing youth team contracts for the following season, but I hadn't heard anything yet. If I was disappointed, I didn't let it show. I watched with pride as my big brother smashed in another hattrick. Surely, he was going to get noticed by the Accies first-team manager soon?

The day before the final the nerves kicked in. Tayla clearly felt the same, so we went to the local park and messed about with a ball, keepy-ups, heads and volleys, just having a bit of fun. There were some younger girls there, some I recognised from our school, others I didn't. They all began to join in and the more fun we had, the more I relaxed. The final wasn't even in my mind when Mum pulled up in the car.

'Isabelle,' she called. 'I think we best be getting back home and getting ready now.' I left a little reluctantly. We were having a lot of fun, but I knew the game tomorrow was so important.

I slept well that night, much better than I thought I would. Waking the next morning was a different matter. The nerves turned my stomach into a washing machine. I found it hard to concentrate, to eat, to do anything. The game wasn't until the evening, so I had to see out the whole day before I could get going.

I watched the highlights of the previous

week's Champions League fixtures with Dad and Jack. The comment was always, 'Accies should be there' or 'One day we will be back there.' It had been a long time since they were the best team in the land, but I felt that we could be, and I hoped that perhaps I might be involved in those big European fixtures one day too. But first, we had to find a way to win the National Championship.

You can't grab hold of your dreams if your hands are holding onto excuses.

A few hours before the game we all met at Falcon Hill. Blackthorpe wanted to give us a rallying speech, meant to inspire us. We listened, but knew it was Miss Hunter who we would give our undivided attention. She had fought for us the whole year whilst Blackthorpe had ignored us.

We weren't about to let him steal her thunder on the eve of the final. We were driven on the school bus to Millbrook House. Through the huge pillars on either side of the neatly kept gravel drive. The bus crunched up the road to the beautiful old school. Big stained-glass windows, with ivy winding its way up the front of the granite building, the main tower lit up by the floodlights that surrounded the main building looked as inspiring as it was imposing. The pitch, bathed in light, had a dewy surface. I knew it had been watered well, so the ball would zip across the surface quickly.

The Millbrook team liked to move the ball fast. But so did I, so I was delighted. We walked through the main lobby, still bustling with students, teachers and officials. This was a very important day for Millbrook House, and they had left nothing to chance. They wanted to win, but they also wanted to put on a show. Excellence was everywhere. Even the gigantic old granite fireplace blazed gold, yellow and red.

We jogged out for our warm-up into the bright lights. I was surprised by the amount of people who were already there. There was a big group of my friends, family and some of the students from Falcon Hill. Being so close, it was easy for them to get there, but you couldn't fail to notice the vast majority of the seating was filled by girls with purple and gold blazers. This was a big deal for them and their school. They expected to do well. They expected to win and win well. Losing to their poor neighbours from down the road was not an option. The non-playing students were expected to show their support, even those who usually went home for the weekends were told they needed to turn up for this final. It was an impressive sight.

There were a lot of coaches and officials on the pitch as we went through our usual routine. One of them I thought I'd recognised. Wearing his purple and gold blazer, with incredibly shiny shoes, it was the man I had spoken to once before. He was walking over towards me.

'Isabelle,' he called. 'Isabelle Harvey?'

'Yes,' I replied quizzically.

'Isabelle, congratulations are in order to you, and your team for a wonderful achievement. Nobody expected your little school to do this well, to reach the final is an extraordinary feat.

'Thank you,' I answered, wondering where this was going.

'Now,' he said a little more firmly. 'I think we can both help each other out here. Millbrook House School is built on excellence. We pride ourselves on our achievements and our results. We demand the best from our students, and they demand the best from us. We don't like losing, especially to a little school from down the road. That would be a little embarrassing, don't you think?'

'I, I guess,' I stumbled. I was confused, I didn't fully understand what the man was telling me.

The man continued,

'You see Miss Harvey, I oversee the sporting scholarships. I look up and down the country and find the very best girls to join our sports programmes; football, athletics, hockey, netball, everything. We bring in the best because we want to be the best, at everything. To get a full scholarship means that your parents wouldn't have to pay a penny towards the school fees, and you would get the best education an English school can offer. Does that sound like something you might enjoy?'

'Yes,' I emphatically replied. My mind was suddenly drawn to an image of my name in gold lettering on my own locker.

'So, here's where you can help us,' the man announced. 'Millbrook House just needs to win today. We need you to,' he hesitated, 'we need you to have an off-day, if you understand what I mean.' He paused as I tried to understand what he meant. 'Think about it,' he said. 'If all goes to plan, next year you could be the captain of the best school team in the country. Have a good game, just not too good,' he said with a smile. 'Oh, and best we keep this little chat to ourselves, ok?' he said as he wandered back to his seat.

I didn't reply. I didn't know what to say. Everything I had dreamed about could be within my grasp. Millbrook House could give me everything I needed, and from there surely one of the top teams' scouts would notice me. But, if I did as he said, I would be letting down my team, my friends, Rachel - who had believed in me all this time. And how could I look Tayla and Zara in the eye again? I was their captain, their leader, we had come so far together. But, I thought, we might lose anyway, even if I played well. But I was confused. I couldn't let my team down. But maybe there was a way that I didn't need to.

I was in a mess, I didn't know what to think. I sat in the enormous dressing room quietly whilst the noise and chat went on all around me. Rachel gave a long speech, all the girls applauded but in truth, I had no idea what she said. I walked out of the changing rooms, down the long corridor and out into the night air. Bright lights and noise were all around me. My eyes were drawn to a girl sitting on one of the benches draped in a blanket. It was Amara, sat there with Miss Fletcher and some of the other girls who weren't involved in the squad. She smiled at me, but I quickly looked away, pretending that I hadn't seen her. I was embarrassed that I had let these thoughts enter my head.

I shook hands with the referee and the opposition captain. I recognised her immediately. She was an excellent defender who had already been called up to represent England at youth team levels.

'That could be me,' I thought as I looked at her MBH captain's armband. Black with golden writing - of course. The floodlights stood high and bright in the sky, and I thought about what it would be like to play here every week. I lost the coin toss, and they chose to kick off. There was little to no wind, so no advantage to be gained there.

The whistle blew and they went at us from the start. All around me, my team was amazing. They tackled well, ran hard and passed beautifully. Millbrook House was on the attack but found it hard to break us down. I ran about a lot, but didn't influence the game much. I passed the ball comfortably, but instead of driving forward, I hesitated. Turning back towards our goal and laying the ball off easily. The Millbrook House girls were giving me no space as they had seen what I did in the semi-final and were worried about what I might do to them. But as the half wore on and they realised that I wasn't influencing the game as they expected I might, and they began to back off slightly. It didn't affect me much. My head was swimming with what their scout had told me. Zara had already given me a few looks; she had realised that something was wrong, but as I was running normally and looked physically fine, she didn't say anything.

Leila didn't hold back. The Latin influence in her blood made her say things I'd have been embarrassed to say!

'Come on Isabelle,' she shouted. 'You need to help us here. We can't get the ball. You keep passing back. Please. We can't do this without you.'

The longer the half went on, the less of an influence I was having, to the point that Zara and Sophia stopped passing to me if we were attacking. I tried to defend a bit better. I figured if I kept the game tight, it would look better. I was desperate to get this scholarship. But then again, what an achievement it would be to win it with Falcon Hill. I wrestled with this thought repeatedly until it was taken out of my hands.

I was caught on the ball, again unsure whether to attack as both Robyn and Poppy moved forward. The Millbrook House midfielder had stepped across me and taken the ball easily. I had lost my balance and ended up sitting on the floor embarrassed. They strode forward with a five to three player advantage, and despite Charley's best efforts, Maya was helpless to prevent a smart cross-shot from being tucked away at the far post. They came at us again and again. I tried to get the ball, but my touch had deserted me, my passing was now all over the place and I couldn't get near their midfielders.

I was lost. Whatever I tried now, failed. Even if I wanted to win this game now it was hopeless. The Millbrook girls were stronger, fitter and better organised. It would have needed a superhuman effort from me at the top of my game. But what they got was probably the poorest half of football I had played all season.

We had held on until a minute before half-time. Millbrook House was on the attack. Since they had scored their opening goal, they had sat back. They didn't over-commit. Still cautious that I might somehow rediscover the kind of form that I had shown on the way to the final. They needn't have worried. Once in possession, one of their skilful midfielders passed beautifully down their line. Ava turned and chased after it, but she had no answer to the sheer pace of the Millbrook winger. She curved in a great cross, Maya couldn't reach it, the ball pinged about in the area and we were unable to clear. I went to close it down, but I was just a fraction too late as a fierce shot struck my hand and went wide. The referee didn't hesitate and blew for a penalty. I was furious. I had no chance to get out of the way, but my emotions suddenly boiled up. The referee wasn't going to change her mind, but I wouldn't stop even when she showed me a yellow card. Tayla sensibly dragged me away before I did something silly. My blood was boiling.

The penalty was dispatched out of the despairing dive of Maya and into the net. Moments later it was half-time. We were done. 2-0 down. I trudged off back to the changing rooms shaking with a mixture of anger at the referee, disappointment in myself, and general frustration that I still didn't know what I should do. I was almost at the door when I heard a low voice.

'Well done Miss Harvey. Good job.'

I turned to see a purple and gold blazer and shiny black shoes walking away.

'What was that all about?' Zara had overheard. 'What did that old stuffed shirt mean?'

'I don't know,' I lied, going bright red in the face, 'never seen him before.' I was embarrassed to tell the truth, especially after that horrible first-half performance.

Rachel tried to pick us up with another amazing speech. This time I did listen. She reminded us that we were more than just a team.

'We have become a family,' she said. 'We have fought through hardships on and off the pitch: the lack of recognition from Blackthorpe, the laughing and name calling. But we are here now. In the final. Win, lose, or draw, we can hold our heads up high. We just need to give our best and that's all we can do.'

'My best,' I thought. This is anything but my best. I was angry at myself. I was letting my teammates down. Even though I wasn't trying to be bad, by letting the thoughts of that scholarship get into my head I was playing poorly.

Zara stood up. It should have been my job, but she recognised that something was up and took control. Despite her fiery temper, Zara was a true team player. 'I wish I was more like her,' I thought.

'It's not over,' she said. 'We have been down and out before. We have come back from 3-0 down. We are fitter, stronger and faster than all of the teams we have played. These are good too, but we will come stronger at the end. If we all keep working hard, we will get chances,' she said, glancing in my direction.

The second half kicked off with us in possession. I was playing a little better but still not great, not by my standards anyway. Zara on the other hand had stepped it up massively. Against her old school, she had a point to prove and was beginning to turn the tide for us. She was winning her tackles, opening up their defence and setting Leila and Poppy away frequently. She had already stung the palms of the Millbrook House goalkeeper and had another shot whistle past the post, when for once I actually won a tackle. Before I could get back to my feet Robyn had taken on the ball and rocketed away down the touchline. Her long deep cross was perfect for Leila who brought the ball down and rolled the ball across the box. Zara was arriving quickly, taking one touch before curling the ball into the bottom corner. It was a great goal and our supporters went crazy. They had begun to sense something was happening and they were getting noisier and noisier.

The Millbrook crowd was stunned into silence, at least for a moment. They hadn't expected anything other than a routine win. But then the noise returned, this time everyone was cheering for both sides.

We were still losing 2-1. But at least now we were making a game of it. I began to get more time on the ball but now we had the problem that time was running out. Poppy, Robyn and even Tess had shots at goal. We were getting closer, but the clock was not our friend. The Millbrook supporters were slowly beginning to celebrate. They thought the game was done. We needed one last chance, but the problem was that the ball was with one of their players deep in our half. She was clearly time-wasting, running down what little time remained on the referee's watch. I moved towards her and as she turned, I stuck out a leg, she lunged to win the ball back and caught me painfully on my foot. The ball rolled harmlessly back to Maya who scooped it up and released Tayla.

She burst forward, passing two surprised Millbrook players. I was back on my feet and chasing hard, but the ball had gone long down the touchline to Poppy. She checked one way, then twisted the other, beating the defender before firing the ball towards the box. Both Zara and I were charging towards the box as Sophia cleverly controlled the ball before rolling it into our paths. I was just ahead of Zara who I knew wanted another goal. I could slow down and let her get there first, but if I did that the defenders might get back. If I got there first, I'd have to take the shot. If I scored, I could lose my dream of that scholarship, but, if I scored, Falcon Hill could go on to win the cup. I had a decision to make, there and then. Did I want that Millbrook House scholarship? The top-level teaching, the opportunities and all the benefits that came with it? Or did I want to create history with this team, with MY team, that I helped put together with my friends?

I had a microsecond to process all that information and make my decision.

Greatness isn't given — it's earned. Every match, every setback, every moment on the pitch shapes the player you become. Dare to believe. Fight for your dreams and rise like a falcon.

Sophia had cleverly rolled the ball into my path on the edge of the penalty area and right then I had to make that decision. In that split second I knew. I leant forward, struck across the ball with my laces as hard as I could and prayed. The ball swerved and dipped. Starting outside the post, before curving back in and striking the angle of the post and crossbar, before bouncing down and into the net.

2-2. We were back in it! Right on full-time as well.

I suddenly realised we now had to navigate extra-time. But now my mind was clear. I knew what I had to do. There was only one option: win. Win the tournament, win the National Cup for Falcon Hill.

Zara looked at me with a quizzical look.

'You ok now?' she asked

I nodded.

'I'll tell you about it all later, but first I need to win this.' I hesitated, 'WE need to win this.' We both smiled. Tayla had come over with a drink for me.

'Drink this Iz,' she said. 'You're gonna need it.'

I ran out for the start of extra time and stood in the centre of a huddle in the middle of the pitch. Millbrook House stood waiting, as did the referee, but at that moment, I didn't care.

'We have come so far,' I said. 'We have fought so hard to get to this point. We have overcome every obstacle that they have put in front of us, and we are still here. This is the biggest game Falcon Hill has ever played, but it's not the end, it's the beginning. It's the beginning of all of our journeys. We will look back at this moment and realise how much this means to every one of us.' I looked at Zara, 'No matter how we got here,' then to Sophia, 'no matter what hardships we have endured to reach this point, we have one chance to create something together that we will never forget. Let's do this!'

We all let out a huge cry of 'FALCON'S' as we broke from the huddle and assumed our positions.

As soon as the referee re-started the match I flew into a tackle, winning the ball cleanly and setting us on the attack. The Millbrook girls were taken aback by the ferocity of my play. I didn't walk, I ran; when I needed to run, I sprinted. My passing was incredible, everything I tried worked. I covered every blade of grass in that first period of extra time. Supporting our attackers when we had the ball, helping the defenders when we didn't. Zara and Sophia were both playing well, and as a result, we began to dominate. I had a half-chance, but their keeper did well to not only stop the ball from going into the goal but to recover and smother the rebound when Poppy was flying in. Moments later, Robyn had another effort, just wide. The longer that extra-time went on, the more likely it seemed that we were going to score.

But Millbrook House were no mugs. They weren't in the final for nothing, and having ridden wave after wave of our attacks, they broke out themselves. We had pushed and pushed to get a goal, fully believing that they were spent, and it was only a matter of time before we won it, but now having lost the ball we were hopelessly exposed. The purple shirts exploded forward and pulled our defenders first left and then right. I had set off in pursuit of the Millbrook captain who had a considerable head start on me, but I had always relied on my pace and was slowly catching her as we flew down the pitch. Charley had done her bit and slowed the attack down, but she couldn't stop them, and as the ball moved to the edge of the area Maya felt she had no option but to come out.

The Millbrook forward, sensing her coming, didn't even look up as she clipped the ball goalwards over Maya's flailing arms and down onto the grass. I was still in a footrace with the Millbrook captain, neck and neck as we flew into the area, both of us flinging ourselves full length at the ball. The Millbrook crowd was breaking into cheers for the imminent goal, when my toe just got under the ball. It was a tiny touch, just a fraction of my boot caught the ball, but it was enough to divert it from my opponent's reach and turn it to the other side of the post.

I lay on the grass, my chest exploding as I

desperately tried to suck in some oxygen. I rolled over to once again come face to face with the Millbrook captain. She was feeling the same.

'That was some challenge,' she said grimacing.

I gave her my best grin as I picked her up off the floor, before clearing the resulting corner with ease.

We pushed on again. Zara passed to Robyn out wide who skipped past two weak challenges. The Millbrook girls were tiring. Our extra training sessions were having an effect. I had recovered from my lung-busting run and was moving forward slowly. Hanging just behind the last defender. Poppy had the ball near the touchline. She dropped her shoulder and ghosted past her defender, looked up and caught my eye before whipping the ball hard and low across the box. There was panic amongst their defenders and a slashed attempt at a clearance only made the ball sit up, right in front of me. As the Millbrook defender regained her feet, I instinctively threw myself for a diving header. In a moment I was transported back to the park with Jack and my friends, playing headers and volleys, and I understood that all that time practicing was for this very moment. I connected perfectly with the ball, and it was past the keeper before she could react.

3-2 Falcon Hill.

The crowd went crazy, well at least our section did. The Millbrook sections looked stunned. They had been 2-0 up and had dominated the first half, but now they were trailing.

They didn't like to lose. They rarely lost.

I ran over to our bench and jumped into Rachel and the others, screaming in excitement. At that moment I couldn't help but notice a man in a purple and gold blazer with shiny black shoes frowning over at us. I did not care. I held up my clenched fist in his direction. This was my team. These were my friends. And this was my school. Whatever happened after this would take care of itself.

There was no way I was letting my football family down.

The game wasn't over, however. Millbrook House was full of champions, and one thing I learned is that true champions never quit. Even when the odds are against you, you never give up. There will always be another chance. Millbrook believed that they would get another chance. They pushed hard but we defended well. Maya made a smart save, but we protected our goal well. The referee had already looked at her watch a couple of times when I intercepted a loose pass on the edge of our box. I knew time was almost up, so I just ran with the ball. I figured that if I had the ball, there was no way they could score. I was being chased hard by a couple of purple shirts, but I knew they couldn't catch me. A third closed me down, but as she got close, I rolled my foot over the ball and poked it between her legs towards the corner, '*my new specialist trick*' I thought. My aim was to take the ball to the corner flag to waste what little time there was left, but I had to adjust my run and move back infield as more defenders closed in on me. I looked around, there were no yellow and blue shirts near me, I had outrun them all, and the rest were too tired to try. Ok, I thought, let's go for the opposite corner, so I made a beeline for there, only to stumble as I was bumped and pushed by the final two defenders. My knee grazed the surface, but somehow I regained my feet, just in time to push off with the ball past the last line of defence. I looked up in amazement as I realised I was now one on one with the goalkeeper.

There was no conflict in my mind this time

as I closed in on goal. I knew exactly what I had to do. The keeper edged out to meet me; I pushed the ball out to my favoured right foot, before curling the ball beyond her outstretched fingers and into the back of the net. I collapsed to my knees as the emotion and sheer exhaustion caught up with me. I could feel tears of joy welling up inside me as I knew that whilst I had lost my chance at the scholarship with Millbrook House School, I had just won the National Championship for little Falcon Hill School.

After what seemed like a joyful lifetime lying on the damp grass, I was engulfed by the rest of my team as the final whistle sounded. Zara typically was the first one to me and must have been the happiest person in the whole stadium. Except perhaps for me.

'So, Miss Harvey,' Tayla asked as we all fell about on the pitch. 'Are you going to tell us what was going on at the start of that game? Because that was an incredible performance at the end.'

I laughed.

'I'll tell you one day,' I said. 'But now we have a trophy to lift.'

I saw the Millbrook House captain standing by herself in the centre of the pitch. She looked crestfallen. I walked over to her.

'Thank you,' I said.

'What for?' she replied looking confused.

'You brought the best out of me today. You are an amazing player, and I hope to have the opportunity to play with you as teammates one day.'

'Thanks, Izzy,' she said. 'I'd rather play with you than against you!' She smiled at me then turned and walked slowly back to her team.

I returned to my team as the trophy presentations were about to get underway. Out of the corner of my eye I saw a familiar, kind-looking man in a yellow and blue tracksuit with a cap jammed hard on his head walking over towards us.

'Hello Isabelle, my name is Walter, Walter Rolland,' he said.

'I know, sir,' I said. I knew exactly who he was. Walter Rolland was the senior men's manager of the mighty Accies. Once one of the best teams in the English Premier League. He had been the manager of the Accies for years, winning the Premier League, FA Cups and a couple of European cups. Everyone loved Walter Rolland, he was Dad and Jack's hero, and now he was here talking to me.

He continued,

'We have been keeping an eye on your brother, Jack, but it seems there is more than one Harvey we need to watch. That was a very impressive performance young lady. We have decided as a club to make our senior women's team a professional team for next season. How would you like to come and try out for us, of course, you can continue your studies at whichever school you choose,' he gestured towards my teammates and then to the hallowed halls of Millbrook House. 'We don't care where you come from, only how much effort and application you put in for the Accies. You, Miss Harvey, are an incredible talent and we want you at the Accies Football Club.' He paused to let his words sink in. 'I think you'd better go and lift that trophy now. Have a think about it and let me know.'

'I don't need to think, sir,' I replied immediately, the words tumbling out of my mouth faster than I could think. 'Of course it is a yes, thank you so much, I'd love to.'

'Thank you, Isabelle,' he said laughing. 'That was a wonderful performance you gave tonight on an important stage. I am very excited to watch both you and your brother take this club back to the very top of the game where it belongs.'

Delighted, I ran off towards my team, and moments later I had the biggest smile ever, as I was lifting the trophy as captain of the best school team in the country.

We were the champions, and best of all, I had done it with my friends.

OTHER TITLES BY
JAMES HEWLETT

JACK HARVEY SERIES
BREAKTHROUGH (1)
BELIEVE (2)

Jackharveybooks.com

ABOUT THE AUTHOR

James Hewlett was born and raised on the beautiful Channel Island of Jersey, surrounded by the sea and rolling green fields. A lifelong sports fan, he's happiest with his dogs by his side, watching football and rugby or cheering on his favourite teams.

As a child, James loved reading, but also playing, watching, and dreaming of football stardom - his hero was none other than Roy of the Rovers. While he never made it to the big leagues, his passion for the game led him to sports writing in 2008, contributing to local newspapers, magazines, and the Jersey Rugby Club, where he also volunteered as a junior coach and media team member.

Following the success of Breakthrough and Believe, James returns with a new series of fast-paced, feel-good football adventures. This time, the spotlight is on Izzy Harvey, sister of local superstar Jack Harvey, as she proves that football isn't just for the boys -it's for everyone.